ALSO BY LINN ULLMANN

Before You Sleep

Stella Descending

Stella Descending

LINN ULLMANN

Translated from the Norwegian
by Barbara Haveland

ALFRED A. KNOPF   NEW YORK   2003

THIS IS A BORZOI BOOK
PUBLISHED BY ALFRED A. KNOPF

Library of Congress Cataloging-in-Publication Data
Ullmann Linn, 1966-
[Når jeg er hos deg. English]
Stella descending / Linn Ullmann ; translated from the Norwegian by
Barbara Haveland.—1st ed.
p.   cm.
"A Borzoi book."
Originally published: Oslo : Tiden Norsk, 2001.
ISBN 0-375-41499-1
I. Title.

PT8951.31.L56N3713 2003
839.8'2374—dc21   200243431

FICTION

9/03

Manufactured in the United States of America
First American Edition

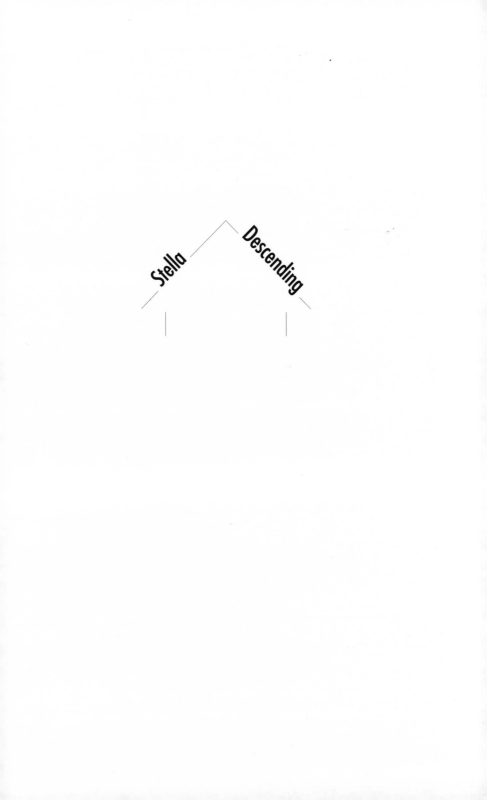

Stella Descending

Video Recording: Stella & Martin
The House by the Lady Falls
8/27/00, 3:25 A.M.

MARTIN: To begin at the beginning: It is summer, almost autumn, a starlit night in the big little city. The hour: between three and four. The plumber's snoring away in the attic. The radio's playing in the kitchen, softly, so as not to wake anyone. Do you hear? It is "Stella by Starlight." You can feel the heat coming after a hot day and the heat coming before a hot day. Everyone in the house is asleep. Hush, now. The children are sleeping. The children are dreaming. Only you and I are awake.

STELLA: Martin.

MARTIN: Yes.

STELLA: I've got something to tell you.

MARTIN: Listen to Stella! She's got something to tell me.

STELLA: Give me a break, Martin.

MARTIN: You want me to give you a break?

STELLA: Yes.

Stella Descending

MARTIN: So we're not going to play like we usually do?

STELLA: No.

MARTIN: You want us to be absolutely one-hundred-percent serious?

STELLA: Yes.

MARTIN: This is Stella. This is my wife. As you can see, Stella is wearing a diaphanous red silk negligee. Would you like me to move in closer? Would you like to see her face? This is Stella's face. Not exactly beautiful, maybe, but—

STELLA: Not beautiful?

MARTIN: No, but actually more beautiful than beautiful. That's what I meant. Not supermodel beautiful, not in-your-face beautiful, but more beautiful than beautiful. What were you going to tell me, Stella?

STELLA: I'd rather be supermodel beautiful. More beautiful than beautiful doesn't mean shit.

MARTIN: Yes it does. It means I love you. You're spoiling the take. . . . Did you get a good look at her face? What did I say? More beautiful than beautiful, right? Okay, now I'm panning down. This is her neck, her long white ballerina neck, with a sharply defined collarbone; that's what I fell for first, her collarbone. And her breasts, of course. You can't see them right now, because she's sitting with her arms crossed, her head to one side, looking kind of forlorn. Don't pay attention, that's just her playing to the camera. She likes everything to revolve around her. I'm particularly fond of her stomach; she tends to hold it in but she can't do it all the time; it sticks out, and I like that; she's not fat—if anything, her women friends say she's skinny, because she's so tall—but she does have a tummy, and it sticks out, and she never buttons the top button on her jeans, which I think is great because that's one less button for me to worry about when I undress her. And now, if I pan downward and if she spreads her legs just slightly, you can see her pussy, pale red like a tomato that's not quite ripe, and if she just spreads her legs a little wider I can take you inside, up inside her, because she's naked under the negligee and there is no lovelier country on earth. Oh, but she refuses to spread her legs a little wider, so instead we'll carry on downward, so you can have a look at the most beautiful feet in all Scandinavia. There they are. Size nine and a half. Red sandals. Burgundy nails. Ten toes I would happily chop off and have for dessert every evening, hold the sugar.

STELLA: Martin.

MARTIN: Yes.

STELLA: Why do we have to do this now?

MARTIN: Why not?

STELLA: Because I want to talk to you.

MARTIN: I thought you were going to bed.

STELLA: No, I wasn't, not exactly. . . .

MARTIN: Then I think we should continue. Now that I've got the camera out; you're here, I'm here.

STELLA: Okay, but then we have to do it right.

MARTIN: What does he care how we do it?

STELLA: What was his name again?

MARTIN: Whose?

STELLA: The insurance broker. What was his name?

MARTIN: I don't know. Can't remember.

STELLA: What was his name . . . ? Get that camera out of
           the way, Martin! Stop filming me! He's not going
           to be interested in my collarbone, or my pussy, *or*
           my toes.

MARTIN: He said "everything of value," right? "Everything
           of value," he said. Okay, this is our house. This is
           our life—

STELLA: Don't change the subject.

MARTIN: Stella, stop interrupting. Okay, it's summer, almost
           autumn, a starlit night in the big little city. It is the
           twenty-seventh of August, two thousand. This is
           our house and this is our living room. This is our
           sofa—stand up, Stella, I want a shot of the sofa—
           and this is our sofa. It's avocado-green, soft,
           Italian. Ten years old, but in good condition. I bet
           we could get fifteen thousand kroner for it today.

STELLA: Yeah, right.

MARTIN: What do you mean, "Yeah, right"?

STELLA: Fifteen thousand kroner for a ten-year-old sofa,
           who's going to believe that—what was his name
           again, the insurance man?—he's never going to
           believe that, Martin. You must be dreaming.

MARTIN: Yeah, that's just what I'm doing. Dreaming! That's
           why we're not in bed asleep at night like other
           people.

STELLA: What would you know about other people?

MARTIN: This is our sofa, our avocado-green Italian sofa,
          gracious, gorgeous, a honey of a sofa. Once upon a
          time, a long time ago, it cost a fortune. If the house
          were to go up in flames it's the thing we would
          miss most. Get the picture? It all started with that
          sofa.

STELLA: We'd miss the kids most.

MARTIN: What?

STELLA: If the house went up in flames, the children are
          what we would miss most.

MARTIN: Yeah, well, okay. As a mother I guess you have
          to . . . but I'm talking about our stuff, Stella. And in
          any case I'm assuming that the kids would be
          rescued, not burnt to a crisp.

STELLA: I'd just like to hear you say it.

MARTIN: What?

STELLA: That none of us is going to be burnt to a crisp.
          That everything's going to be okay.

MARTIN: Everything's going to be okay.

STELLA: Good.

MARTIN: Now, what were you going to tell me, Stella?

(I)

FALL

I have two large ears.

I have two large ears shaped like Italian portals, but I don't use them anymore. First I went deaf in one ear, then I went deaf in the other. Worse things have happened.

I put my knitting in my bag and tilted my head back, looking up. They were like two dolls up there on the roof, he with his Bible-black locks, she in a yellow-and-red dress. Back and forth along the edge. Swaying back and forth. I shouted at them to get down from there. There are plenty of ways to die without landing on other people's heads. As a pedestrian you ought to be insured against that sort of thing. Then they stopped and looked down. My, how that must have made their heads spin. And then they hugged. Although I don't know. Was it a hug? If you ask me, it looked more like a sort of tussle. She was pulling away and he was hanging on. Or maybe he was pulling away and she was hanging on. And then it happened: She lost her footing and fell. Or he pushed her, and she fell. It's hard to say just what happened. But she fell, that's for sure. And I felt my stomach sink. One time, I thought I saw a plane fall out of the sky. And I felt my stomach sink that time too. I squeezed my eyes tight shut and waited for the thud. For a moment there I forgot I was deaf.

Corinne

The other night on the streetcar, I spotted a man I thought I knew. He was sitting very still, a few seats in front of me, gazing out the window. There wasn't much to see out there; the streets were deserted and it was dark and miserable, just the odd car swishing by. No one in the street, just flurries of snow chased by rain, and the wet white light of the streetlamps.

I saw him first from the back. He was wearing a brown leather jacket, his hair was thick and black—a handsome man, I thought, a man who walks tall and never stumbles. Just for a second I thought I saw a little girl dressed in red on the seat next to him, but then I gave my head a shake. What was I thinking? There was no child there. As if there would be, in such weather and at that time of night. There was no one on the streetcar but him and me—and the driver, of course. The man stood up and headed for the door at the front. We were approaching a stop.

"Martin Vold," I called out softly. "Is that you?"

The man turned around. His face was not familiar. I noticed two beady green eyes and a scar on his chin.

"You must be mistaken," he said, as the doors opened. "That's not me."

"No," I said, "that's not you. But good night, anyway, and watch your step out there. The pavement's slippery."

"Thanks, you too," said the man. "Good night."

It hasn't even been six months since the last time I had anything to do with him. That was at the beginning of September last year. The evening before Stella's funeral I called on him at home in Hamborgveien, up by the Lady Falls. We sat down at the large dark-brown dining table, and there we passed the night. He asked me to keep my voice down, so as not to wake the children. He did most of the talking. I asked questions. It's what I'm good at—asking questions—and it occurred to me while we were sitting there that it was as if we were making up a story together, he and I, and that as we went on, the story of what really happened was slipping through my fingers. In my job I'm used to that sort of thing—stories slipping through my fingers, I mean—but that doesn't make it any less disappointing. I watch, I listen, I intuit, I know. But I have no power over what happens. I cannot prevent tragedies.

Where to begin? The murder itself—if it was murder, that is—took place on August 27, 2000. But I will begin with the footnote, the historical background, if you like.

On February 23, 1934, a thirty-two-year-old man met his death when he fell from atop an apartment building on Frogner-plass in Oslo. The man whose life ended in this way was a popular, good-looking, and gifted actor with a bright future in front of him. He was known for playing horses with the chairs in the Hotel Continental's Annen Etage, bouncing around the restaurant to the strains of the "Ryttermarsjen." Four days later, Johan Peter Bull, the National Theater's dramatist and secretary, noted in his diary that he feared there might be trouble at that evening's performance of *When We Dead Awaken*. There was talk of plans to disrupt the play with boos and catcalls, in protest against one of the National Theater's most beguiling actresses, who was currently winning great acclaim for her portrayal of Irene. Some felt this actress was partly to blame for her young colleague's death, inasmuch as the two had been having an affair. The police turned out in force, but the performance went off without incident.

In the audience that evening was a young man, a farmer's son named Elias Vold. This was Martin Vold's paternal grandfather. Elias hailed from Sweden, where his parents ran an ostrich farm in Sundbyberg, outside Stockholm, but when he was only fifteen the lad was forced to move from this farm to another one, in Høylandet. This experience—of leaving his mother and father in Sweden to go live with his two uncles in Norway—was to leave its mark on him for the rest of his short life. His uncles, who were cattle and sheep farmers, took turns beating him every night, and he had to work hard for his bread. He missed his parents, but they could no longer support him; like their fellow ostrich farmers elsewhere in the world, they had been hit hard by the ostrich crash of 1918. The crash followed a global swing in fashion; ladies everywhere had lost the taste for hats trimmed with ostrich feathers. It was the first of three great tragedies to befall the Vold family. I would even go so far as to say that had fashions in millinery been more stable, none of these three tragic events would have occurred and I would not be sitting here today, in the winter of 2001, with an unexplained death on my hands.

The once-thriving ostrich farm in Sundbyberg was sold, taken over by two rival companies, Svensk Bio and Skandia, who joined forces on this one occasion to build Råsunda Filmstad, home of the legendary film studios. Here, the filmmakers Victor Sjöström and Mauritz Stiller worked alongside such stars as Tora Teje, Lars Hanson, Anders de Wahl, Karin Molander, and Hilda Borgström. Greta Garbo turned in an impressive performance in *Gosta Berling's Saga* in 1924, "giving us hope for the future," to quote the ecstatic critic in *Svenska Dagbladet*. I can well imagine how Elias must have cursed the day his parents decided to put their money in ostriches rather than the movies.

Be that as it may. As soon as he came of age, Elias ran away from his two uncles and from his sweetheart, Harriet, who was known as the loveliest lass in all of Høylandet. An ostrich feather was all he took with him when he boarded the bus that would carry him from Høylandet to Skogmo station. He then caught the train to Trondheim and there another, going to Oslo.

And so it happened that Elias was in the audience that evening in February 1934 to see *When We Dead Awaken* with the beguiling actress in the part of Irene—undisturbed, fortunately, by catcalls or any other show of disapproval. Later that evening, Elias wrote Harriet a letter in which he told her about the play, the catcalling that had failed to transpire, the rumors of an unhappy love affair between the two Ibsen interpreters, and the young actor's fall from the top of the apartment building in Frogner. And one other thing: It would be some time before he returned to Høylandet, he wrote. He could well understand if Harriet did not feel like waiting for him, but he wanted to try his luck on the stage, possibly even in movies—yes, movies for sure. Who knew what might lie in store for a young man like himself? He closed the letter with a few well-chosen lines from *When We Dead Awaken*, since it was precisely during that very performance at the National Theater, on February 27, 1934, that he— inspired, as it were, by Henrik Ibsen—had the idea of breaking it off with his sweetheart in Høylandet and embarking on a new life as a star of stage and screen.

Elias had another passion, too—namely, for lying down on railway tracks, in particular on the line between Tøyen and Grefsen. He would try to see how long he could lie there without being run over. Unfortunately, one day he lay there too long and was killed: sliced in half. Råsunda Filmstad was history. His body was sent back to Høylandet: this time, again, by train, from Oslo to Trondheim, where another train carried it to Skogmo; there it was loaded aboard the bus to Høylandet. It was a quiet funeral. His parents were dead, and his uncles couldn't have cared less. Only his sweetheart, Harriet, now eight months heavy, with tears streaming becomingly down her plump cheeks—only she was there to bid him a last farewell.

After the ceremony, Harriet remained on her knees at Elias's graveside, whispering into the pile of earth, her swollen belly clearly visible beneath her winter coat, her long fair braid hanging down her back. It was dusk. An icy winter wind tugged at the posy of flowers she had laid on the coffin. She made no move to get up, just stayed on her knees, her head almost in the grave itself, whispering, hands fluttering. No one had the heart to disturb her, although a few passersby did stop to stare from a distance. Naturally, everyone was wondering what she could possibly have to say now to this man who had let her down so badly in life.

Five weeks later, Harriet gave birth to a bouncing baby boy. For the record, I have to confess that Harriet's bouncing baby boy does not interest me in the slightest. I have tried to picture his face, his life, his passions, even, but to no avail. All I can say is that he was named Jesper, that he went on to honor his Swedish grandparents by resurrecting on a grand scale their dream of Scandinavian ostrich farming, and that years later he started up the first ostrich farm in Norway, at Høylandet. There! That's Jesper's story! Oh, yes, one other thing: Back in the fifties, Jesper married Nora, and with her he had a son: Martin.

Winter 1990. Our story proper begins about now, on a day in late January, let us say. Here's picture number one: We are standing outside an apartment building in the Frogner district of Oslo, scene of the young actor's tragic death in 1934. In the picture you can see a hydraulic lift extending upward to a closed window on the ninth floor. Atop the lift is a platform, on the platform sits a spanking-new avocado-green sofa, and on the sofa sits Martin, with a big smile on his face. I don't know whether you have noticed, but behind the closed window on the ninth floor, half hidden behind a pale blue curtain, a young woman is waiting.

The name of the woman behind the blue curtain on the ninth floor is Stella. On a sunlit evening just over ten years after Martin climbs through her window, she will fall from that selfsame building in Frogner. The descent, from the moment she loses her footing until she hits the ground, will take two seconds. Two seconds: no more, no less. It is these two seconds on which I shall endeavor here to shed some light.

I am a special investigator with the Violent Crimes division of the Oslo police department. The sign on my office door says C. DANIELSEN. The C is for Corinne. I have no friends; my coworkers call me Corrie the Chorus because of my theatrical background. In my former life I was a ventriloquist and puppet maker. At one time I even had my own puppet theater. My pièce de résistance was a number featuring fifty puppets, a very fair representation of the entire cast of *La Bohème*.

My real gift, however, is that I get an ever so slight twinge in my stomach whenever I come face-to-face with a killer. Call it intuition. I can also tell when I'm on the brink of a confession and when I am not. This is one of those cases in which I never did get a confession. The case was dropped due to lack of evidence. Martin took his red-clad daughter, Bee, by the hand and walked away, vanishing from my sight until that winter's night in Oslo, when he turned up again on that streetcar—or so I thought. He got off scot-free.

Hence these words.

Amanda

Listen! Sometimes at night, when I'm in bed, Mamma is here with me. Okay, not *right* here but close by. And sometimes she talks, not to me and not to Bee, but to someone else: Martin, maybe, or the old geezer. She doesn't know I can hear her. Martin doesn't want to hear, and the old geezer is deaf, so I suppose you could say she's talking to nobody.

A few years ago, Mamma got sick and kept saying to herself, Better not fall now, better not fall. She used to say the same thing to me: Better not fall now. And to Bee: Better not fall now. I didn't know what she meant. She was lying in bed flat on her back, and Bee and I were standing with our feet flat on the floor, and there she was saying we better not fall. You can't fall when you're already lying in bed, I told her. She said it was just a figure of speech. She didn't mean it literally. But then some years went by and she fell anyway. Literally. And that was that. I don't think people should go around using figures of speech all over the place if they don't mean them literally. I must remember to tell Mamma that next time she's close by.

That time when she was sick we thought she was going to die, but she didn't. She got better and went back to work and said things I didn't like: that she was living on borrowed time. When she was in the hospital, she asked me to read to her. Books and newspapers. She asked me to read *Moby-Dick*, because she felt you couldn't die without having read *Moby-Dick*. We never managed to finish it. She couldn't take it after a while. There came a point where all she wanted me to read were the real estate ads in *Aftenposten*. "Bright three-room apartment in quiet street, with balcony," that sort of thing. That cheered her up. You'll have to go and look at that one, she'd say, so I would, and afterward I would tell her all about the three rooms and the balcony, and about the light.

Bee is my little sister. She's a quiet kid. Quiet, not stupid. She listens and she takes it all in. I tell her Mamma fell off a roof. Listen, Bee, I say. Mamma fell off a roof, Mamma's falling still. She falls and falls and never hits the ground. That's what we say. We say that Mamma is falling little by little, day by day, kind of in bits: first a finger, then an eye, and then a knee, and then a foot, then a toe, and then another toe. It takes longer that way. Not all of Mamma at once, *crash-bang-wallop* onto the ground. Mamma with her long fair hair, all mussed up. Mamma is beautiful. I mean was. I mean is, was; I don't really know. She has one blue eye and one violet eye, burgundy toenails, yellow summer dress, and around her neck a silver locket that Granny left her. I was her daughter, the older one, and I am the one who painted her toenails burgundy. That was a long time ago. Mamma sat at one end of the white double bed, with two white pillows at her back, the window was open onto the garden, and the sun was shining. I sat at the other end, polishing her toes. That was when Mamma said, "I have the most beautiful feet in Scandinavia." Just so you know. My mother, the dying, the dead, has the most beautiful feet in Scandinavia.

A while ago, Mamma said to Martin, "If the whole thing weren't so goddamn depressing, I 'd be laughing at you now." And then she laughed.

Stella Descending

Sometime I'll have to tell you about Mamma's laugh. That, too, would come a little at a time. First a tiny chuckle, like one red marble rolling across the floor, then a slightly bigger marble, and then a whole bagful of marbles, *crash-bang-wallop*, all the marbles rolling across the floor at once.

Outside this door everything's in an uproar. In here it's quiet. This is Bee's room. I take off my shoes. We're already dressed for the funeral, red summer dresses and white shoes. I wanted a black dress, but that idiot Martin said no. I lie down on the bed next to Bee, sniff her hair, her skin; "It's okay," I say.

Bee doesn't cry. She is very quiet. Plays with my hair a bit. I wish she would cry or something.

I'm going to lie here for a while, next to Bee. "Shut your eyes," I say. "She's close by."

"Do you think so?" she whispers.

"Put out your hand to her," I say, "and she'll give it a squeeze."

There are lots of things I don't tell Bee. For example, (1) I have three boyfriends who are crazy about me; (2) Everything the minister says today will be a bunch of lies; and (3) In the depths of his dark heart, Martin, her father, our mother's husband, furniture salesman and ostrich king, is actually a wicked sorcerer.

So this is my story. There's no happy ending. My mother is dead. I am fifteen. My name is Amanda. It means, *She who is worthy of love.*

Axel

There are certain places where I feel at home. Perhaps "feel at home" is not the right way to put it; better to say there are certain places where I feel at home with myself. By which I mean, external landscapes that accord with my own inner landscape. I come to a place, and it feels as if I have been there a hundred times before. Everything fits: the proportions, the colors, the distances, the clear sky above, the light. I come to a place where I find I am breathing, that I can breathe, that I am in harmony with my surroundings. I can't explain it any other way. It's not something I have experienced often in my life. I am not usually in harmony with my surroundings. In fact, I detest my surroundings, and my surroundings detest me.

Today I have to attend Stella's funeral. After the funeral I will pick up my old blue Volkswagen Beetle, my third, from the repair shop. That Beetle is almost as rickety as I am, and like me it is constantly succumbing to a host of peculiar ailments. I'll take it for a spin. It will do us both good, the Beetle and me. This evening, when I get back home, I shall have entrecôte of venison, washed down with a bottle of Châteauneuf-du-Pape. Sometimes I light a candle for my wife, Gerd. Today I shall light a candle for Stella too. Before going to bed, I will take two sleeping tablets and possibly listen to part of a piano sonata by Schubert.

It is my hope—a thought I have every morning, not least this one—that this will be the last day of my life.

MY HOME FOR the past thirty years has been a three-room apartment in Majorstuen. There is no sense of harmony between the apartment in Majorstuen and myself. I have always considered the place temporary. The rooms are furnished haphazardly, I have never purchased a stick of furniture myself, and when I moved here after Gerd died, I brought nothing with me from the old house—nothing except the gilt mirror that now hangs in the hall. I just sold everything else and handed over the key.

Every Thursday a woman about fifteen years my junior comes to clean the place. No, not a woman. That's not the right word. An old hag, that's what she is. An offense to the eye. I don't know why I ever gave her the job, and I'm sure she has no idea why she took it. It was all so long ago there's no sense brooding over it now. My only comfort is that she detests me as much as I detest her. Which does not mean we are not utterly civil to each other. I call her Miss Sørensen, even though no one calls anyone Miss these days, and she calls me Grutt. That is my name. I am Axel Åkermann Grutt. I happen to know that the old hag's first name is Mona, and that as a young woman she held some minor position in the Oslo tax department. So—only to myself of course—I call her Miss Money Sørensen, or simply Money.

Because she is a grasping old hag, and because she sometimes steals from me—ten kroner here and ten kroner there—although I never say anything. That would put us both in an untenably awkward situation. I have lots of other names for her as well, but some things I shall keep to myself till my dying day, which can't be too soon. Besides, a bit of decorum is surely in order, even when it comes to Money. Not that she has ever shown any, coming to work in those short skirts of hers with her garish lipstick and woolen panty hose. If I had any trace of that highly fashionable quality *empathy*, I might well feel sorry for her, even to the point of not begrudging her the petty sums she steals from me each week. Money is old, weary, and pathetic, but like most women she imagines that short skirts and red lips will conceal her wretchedness rather than lay it bare.

Money is one person I see regularly. The other, apart from Stella, who is being buried today—she fell or was pushed off a roof on Frognerplass—is Stella's fifteen-year-old daughter, Amanda. She often pays me a visit. It used to be she only came with her mother, but eventually she started coming on her own, too, and despite the fact that we don't have much to say to each other and despite the fact that I don't really like children—I think they're overrated, to be honest—we spend a few hours in each other's company now and then. Sometimes we play cards, I have taught her to play Høff, a game for two players using two packs of cards. She is also impressed by my feeble magic tricks, which is rather flattering. I used to be quite good. Amanda has pale fine-drawn features. She tells me she likes video games. I tell her I like Ferris wheels. It would never occur to either of us to speak of our loneliness.

Money and Amanda. There you have the circle of my acquaintance among the living. I could perhaps add to this list the blank-eyed young woman at the newsstand on the corner where I buy my papers. After all, I do see her every day. And speak to her, too. I say good morning and tell her which newspapers I would like (the same five, always), and then, after the same correct sum has passed from my hand to hers, I say goodbye. But by definition, an acquaintance ought at least to recognize one's face, and the young woman at the newsstand has never recognized mine.

I GAVE UP SMOKING five years ago. I took a course, the strategy of which was to get the participants to dislike cigarettes, something that had previously given them pleasure. Every time I had the urge to light a cigarette, they told me that, old geezer that I am, I should chew on a stick of licorice instead. A licorice stick! Inevitably, all we ever talked about at every session was what a struggle it had been to get through another week without cigarettes and whether we had given in or "cracked," in the parlance of the course.

Let us get one thing clear: I did not attend this course of my own free will. I was ordered to do so by my family physician, my only friend of some thirty years' standing in fact (and, at one time, Stella's boss), Dr. Isak Skald. He told me if I continued smoking I would die. It was, as I told him, hardly a sound argument since (1) I greatly enjoyed smoking and (2) I had nothing against dying. The sooner the better, said I. But Skald, some years my junior, was so determined to preserve my old carcass, this thing he was prepared to count as a life, that I was robbed, as it were, of my own will, leading me to wonder whether I had ever had a will of my own at all. At any rate, his was the stronger, which was vexing enough in itself. It would prove to be of little comfort when Skald himself up and died of a heart attack not a year later, at the tender—to me—age of seventy-five. By then the joy was gone. Skald had taken it with him to the grave. (He had told me once, a long time ago, that he found joy in his wife Else's hands. It was almost unbelievable, he said, that a woman's two hands could change everything, all ideas of a well-ordered bachelor existence, all self-elected solitude, all disdain for matrimonial ties; thanks to Else's hands and the constant longing for Else's caresses, he no longer had any desire to go on living alone in his apartment with two aging mistresses lodged at a safe distance, according to his original intent. Instead, he wanted to spend the rest of his days with Else.)

Don't get me wrong: I did try to take up smoking again. Indeed, I smoked plenty of cigarettes during the reception following Skald's funeral; I stood in a corner of Skald's lovely bright living room, virtually devouring cigarettes and canapés and drinking beer. Then out of nowhere Else, a tall woman, six feet if she was an inch, sidled up to me, her lips at my ear. (That day, Else had turned in an exceptionally good performance as the grieving widow: dignified, composed, and warm, with becomingly red-rimmed eyes. She looked younger than her sixty-four years. Her fifteen-year marriage to Skald had been her third. His predecessors had also died, so she knew the role of widow, though not having played it for some time.)

"You know Isak made it a point of honor to get you to give that up," she whispered, pointing to the cigarette between my fingers. "He'd be quite beside himself if he knew."

I looked at her face, her glistening eyes, her gray suit, her hands—two broad gold bands on the ring finger of the left one, Skald's ring and her own.

"Your husband, my friend, would not be *beside* himself, as you put it, wherever he is now," I muttered.

"That may be," she whispered, "but *I'm* still here, and *I'm* beside myself. I'm beside myself." She dropped her gaze, wiped away a tear, and said, "And I think it's silly of you to start smoking again after being off it for so long and having done so well."

(A marvelous woman, I remember thinking to myself; it did not surprise me when she married again some months later.) Then she raised one of those hands that had once given my friend Dr. Isak Skald such joy and plucked the cigarette from my lips.

"For my sake," she whispered, kissed me on the forehead, and stubbed out the cigarette in the ashtray. Then she moved on to the next guest who had come to pay his last respects.

I MET STELLA ten years ago at Ullevål Hospital. She was a nurse, I was a patient. For some reason—this is one of the most remarkable things that has ever happened to me—every day this young woman would come to my room and perch on the edge of my bed, chattering on about everything and nothing (not least about Martin, whom she had just met and fallen in love with) as if it were her honest wish to be my friend. I say again that I have no idea why she might have desired my company or what she may have seen in me, an old man with one foot in the grave; sometimes I wonder whether she saw me at all, sitting there at my bedside: young, dressed in white, nattering on.

My stay in the hospital was a fairly lengthy one. Skald had persuaded me to have an operation. I won't go into details. The old carcass was falling apart. The pain was exquisite. I say exquisite because God, if he exists, is brutally inventive. The litany of agonies and afflictions that beset the human spirit and body is, I think, exquisite in its candor. God glamorizes nothing—everything hurts, everything breaks down, there is no mistaking the way things are going. Dying is one thing, a relief, I think. But growing old is hard work.

Stella Descending

At that time, ten years ago, Stella was working in the geriatric unit, but later she switched to treating the dying, primarily cancer patients, at the Radium Hospital.

Her face. In my mind's eye I see it all the time but as if in a dream, very close, right up against my own—still I can't describe her features because the face keeps changing.

She reminded me of my only daughter, Alice, whom I haven't seen since my wife died in '69 (Alice felt I was to blame for her mother's death, that somehow my "selfish, harsh, tyrannical nature" had caused the cancerous growth in Gerd's stomach). Stella had the same tremendous lust for life as Alice, the same proud bearing. I'm not talking here of the sort of beauty that comes from perfect facial features or a shapely figure—neither Alice nor Stella could be described as beautiful in the traditional sense—but a beauty that springs from physical grace. Even as a little girl Alice could take my breath away just by running down the street toward me, arms outstretched. So too with Stella. I can see her now, way down at the other end of a hospital corridor or sitting on the edge of my bed: an angular young woman with broad shoulders, narrow hips, small round breasts, and lively, expressive hands. She was very tall, slim, and slightly round-shouldered—a princess on stilts. Sometimes she would sweep through a room with all her usual style and grace, other times with a less-expected, faltering sort of charm.

I've always been fascinated by Ferris wheels. I like to stand and watch them from a distance. Or look at pictures of old ones, in Coney Island, Vienna, London, Chicago, Tokyo. Even the garish little wheels of traveling fairs have their allure. Of course these days it would never occur to me to get onto one and spin slowly through the air, round and round. Not anymore. I am too old. My father took me up in a Ferris wheel once, and on that day he told me we were distantly related to the American engineer George Washington Ferris, who invented it.

When Alice was a little girl I took her on the beautiful Ferris wheel in Vienna. I remember the snow falling, the lights, her gleeful laughter, and the way she stood up in the gondola, stretching her arms into the air. The last time I dared to go up in one was with Stella, at the Tivoli Gardens in Copenhagen. We happened to bump into each other on the street. She was in town for a conference on care of the terminally ill, and I was there to . . . well . . . to go to Tivoli. She was most surprised to see me outside her hotel.

"I can't believe it!" she said. "You're in Copenhagen, Axel?"

I replied that I was indeed and often had business in Denmark (I believe that I did in fact use the word *business* as if it were the most natural thing in the world).

She said it was nice to see me, that she actually had quite a busy day ahead of her, but surely we could find time for a cup of coffee. I said, "Couldn't we go to Tivoli instead and try the Ferris wheel?" She looked as if she had been struck by a bolt out of the blue. Or, rather, she looked at me as if I had just fallen out of the blue, to land outside her hotel in Copenhagen at two-thirty in the afternoon. Evidently it had never occurred to her that I might be the sort of man who frequented amusement parks.

"You sat so still, Axel, with your big hand over mine, and when we reached the highest point you said, 'Look, Stella! Look!'"

"And you hardly dared to open your eyes, couldn't understand what I saw in this form of entertainment."

WHEN I SAW STELLA for the first time, way down at the other end of the hospital corridor, dressed all in white, so purposeful, and with that—how shall I say?—singing inside her, I was put in mind of the time Alice was to be married. When I met her, Stella was in her mid-twenties and she and Martin had just started living together. Alice was also in her mid-twenties when, for some unfathomable reason, she decided to get married. I was to lead her to the altar and hand her over to an estimable fiancé, whose name I'm glad to say I have forgotten. He was a tall, dark, bespectacled man whose only good trait was that he always agreed with the last person to speak, seldom forcing his own ideas and opinions—whatever these might have been—on others. If there was one man about whose thoughts I had no wish to be enlightened, it was Alice's fiancé. There are torments even I have been spared! Anyway, I collected my white-clad daughter at her studio apartment . . . how many years ago was that? It would have been in '63, six years before Gerd died—I picked her up at her tiny apartment and made room for her in my blue Volkswagen Beetle, the one that was to give up the ghost in the seventies but at that time still shone like the sun. We drove to the church. Alice was quiet. Her veil kept falling over her face and she blew it away in exasperation, as if it were the long hair she had never had. I chatted dutifully about the weather and mentioned that her mother was looking forward to the party afterward; she had left for the church a half hour earlier to check that the flowers had been arranged just so, and the whole house was filled with the glorious smell of roast reindeer—that sort of thing.

"Huh!" said Alice distractedly as we were turning up toward the church.

"What's the matter, Alice?" I asked.

"Maybe this is all a big mistake," said Alice.

"Oh, Alice, come now," I said, opening my door and then walking around to open hers.

She gathered up her skirts, aggressively almost, pushed her veil back from her face, and set off at a jog toward the church. Although the sun was shining that day, a stiff breeze was blowing. She turned back to me and shouted, "Come on, Pappa! Everybody's here. There's nothing to do but march right on in there!"

Outside the church door, she let her skirts fall around her. I straightened her veil. She gave me a defiant look, and I stroked her cheek.

"You don't like him much, do you?" she whispered.

"Alice, it's you who's marrying him, not me."

The music struck up, the doors were thrown open, and my daughter and I began our walk down the aisle. All the wedding guests rose to their feet; at the altar stood the estimable fiancé, arranged with the bridesmaid and best man. All eyes were on us. Alice slackened her pace and leaned toward me, her lips to my ear.

"The problem is, Pappa, that the only thought in my head at this moment is that five years from now I'm going to want a divorce. I won't be able to stand that guy for more than five years."

We continued down the aisle as Alice whispered these words in my ear. I leaned toward her and muttered that this was not the right time to be discussing her possible divorce. Then she came to a complete halt. A faint murmur ran through the congregation, a ripple of uneasy curiosity. Alice came to a complete halt and whispered in my ear.

"The problem, Pappa, is not that *you* don't like him. The problem is that *I* don't like him! I think he's an arrogant jerk. Look at him! Look at him standing there with that pompous look on his face, waiting to marry me. I can just feel it in my bones, Pappa, this is going to be no fun at all!"

We stood there in the aisle, eyes fixed on her fiancé, who was himself starting to look puzzled. We spent a long time staring at him. Eventually I leaned toward my daughter.

"Well then, Alice, there's only one thing to do," I whispered.

She looked at me and gave me her most dazzling smile, and we turned right around. We turned and paced back just as solemnly as we had made our way down the aisle, just as slowly in the opposite direction, away from the altar, away from the estimable fiancé, toward the church door. In sheer consternation, the verger opened the door, letting us out into the light. And before the congregation had collected itself, we were back inside my blue Beetle.

"Okay, where to now?" I asked my daughter.

Alice just laughed.

"Oh, Pappa, I do love you," she said, laying her head on my shoulder as I started the car and drove off. "I love you so very, very much."

Today I'm off to church again—or, rather, to the crematorium—this time on account of Stella. It's a relief to know that the next funeral I attend will be my own. Stella was afraid of death, which is possibly why she worked with it day in, day out. I don't know. She was young. She had children: two girls. Amanda and then Bee, a quiet little thing she had with the conceited ass to whom she was married.

. . .

"But you don't like anyone, Axel; everybody's either an old hag, or detestable, or disreputable, or an offense to the eyes—and what was it you called Martin?"

"A conceited ass."

"How come? Give me one good reason."

"He's reckless."

"So are you, Axel, in your own way."

"He's dishonest."

"And what does that make you, the soul of truth?"

"He's not good to you."

"There are plenty of people worse off than me."

I do not fear death. I learned early on from my father that the right to die by one's own hand is the most fundamental of human freedoms. There is always a way out. I have known this since I was a boy: There is always a way out! And my father actually did put an end to it all, taking my mother with him. Whether he did so deliberately, I cannot say, although he probably did. Long after we children had grown up and left home, before the war, they went missing in the Trollheimen Mountains and weren't found until spring. They had been caught in an avalanche, or so it was said. They left no money. My sisters inherited our mother's few dresses and cheap jewelery. I inherited a chandelier. When Gerd and I got married, she hung the chandelier in the living room. She thought it was beautiful. She said it lit up both the room and itself, unlike me, she said; I didn't light up the room, myself, or anything else for that matter. I remember her sitting on the floor in her blue-checked dress with a yellow cardigan around her shoulders and her hair in a braid, sitting under the chandelier and gazing up at it for hours on end. One night after she had fallen asleep, I crept out of bed and downstairs to the living room, where I climbed onto a chair and pulled off one crystal after another until the chandelier was stripped bare. The next morning, Gerd demanded an explanation. I did not feel I owed her one and said as much. I still have the crystals, sealed up in a box in the cellar, next to the barrel organ.

Stella did not want to die. She would never have fallen off a roof, just like that. As a child, you are always falling. Then you stop. Your morals go on falling, of course, but you yourself stop. Very rarely do you see a grown woman or man fall down—in the street, for example, or on a streetcar—and the odd time this does happen it is extremely unpleasant for both the person who has fallen and the one looking on: a shared loss of balance. Then you grow old and you start falling again. These days I'm forever falling down. My knees give way beneath me. I slip on the ice. I want to go in one direction; my feet go in another. When I venture out onto the street, this is what I fear most: falling down. That I'll fall and break something, to say nothing of making myself the laughingstock of anyone happening by. Stella would not have jumped, either. Not from her children. What she could have been doing up on that roof is a mystery to me. He must have forced her to go up there. They were reckless, those two, Stella and Martin, just like children. Daring and bullying each other. Clinging to and pushing each other away. Maybe it was only a matter of time before one shoved the other over the edge.

Amanda

Other things I don't tell Bee: For example, (4) I call my boyfriends Snip, Snap, and Snout. They don't know I do. They don't know I have more than one boyfriend, either. Snip doesn't know there's a Snap and Snap doesn't know there's a Snout and Snout doesn't know there's a Snip or a Snap. When I was thirteen I had no breasts and no boyfriends. Marianne had breasts— but then she was a year older so that wasn't so surprising. Marianne was my best friend at that time. Once, she took off all her clothes in Mamma's room. She took off all her clothes and stood in front of Mamma's big mirror, and I stood behind her and we gazed in awe at her breasts, her skin, and her lovely long fair hair and her little round tummy and her butt and legs. I told her if I was a boy I'd definitely want to fuck her. That's what I said, but I was thinking that what I really felt like doing was running a finger down the side of her body, following the soft line that curved in at her waist and out at her hips. Marianne stood in front of Mamma's big mirror, stark naked in front of Mamma's big mirror, and then all at once she gave a little jump, a jump for joy, sort of, and the words just blurted out of her: *Oh my god, I'm gorgeous!*

I don't think she meant to say it out loud, because her face went bright red and she scrambled back into her T-shirt and panties as quick as she could.

I'm fifteen now, and I look pretty good too, not as good as Marianne but not bad at all. That time in front of Mamma's big mirror, I didn't look good. Sometimes I would put on a lot of sweaters, one on top of the other, so nobody could see I didn't have breasts. When the boys see me, I thought, all they'll say is, There goes a girl who's all wrapped up. Not: There goes a girl who's got no breasts. Since then I've come to the conclusion that when they saw me the boys didn't think anything one way or the other.

I tell Bee, who's lying here in bed beside me, that Mamma falls and falls and never hits the ground. And while she's falling she sees the strangest things and she meets the strangest people and creatures. Birds, for example, flying south. But birds don't fall, they fly. There is a difference. She meets a squirrel that has fallen out of a tree and a cod that has been fished out of the water by a boy and then tossed, half alive, half dead, onto dry land. I explain to Bee that it's exactly the same thing, as misfortunes go, for a cod to be pulled out of the sea as for a squirrel to fall out of a tree. I cover us both with a blanket. Maybe Mamma will meet Granny too, I say; God must have kicked Granny out of heaven a long time ago, she was so grumpy and tight-lipped.

Axel

It is an annoying fact of life that Money Sørensen always lets herself into my apartment at the most inconvenient time. It's true that we agreed on every Thursday at ten, and it's true that she turns up every Thursday at ten, but *for me* Thursday at ten is and always will be an inconvenient time! Exactly thirty years ago, when we came to the arrangement whereby she would come here on that day at that time to clean and tidy this place, I felt as if I were committing myself under duress. It would have suited me better if we had agreed, for example, on every Friday at one o'clock, at which time I am always out for a stroll. Every Monday at twelve would also have been quite suitable, since I usually spend a few hours downtown at Deichmann's library around that time. Even Wednesdays after eleven would have been fine, Wednesday being my day for errands in town: shopping for food, going to the bank, that sort of thing. But Thursday at ten is, and always will be, the most unsuitable time imaginable. Unforeseen things are always happening on Thursdays. Today, for example—today I have a funeral to attend, so I have to take a bath and get changed. Isak Skald was also buried on a Thursday. But I'm not just talking about funerals. Young Amanda often looks in on a Thursday—she finishes school early that day—and the last thing I want when Amanda pays me a visit is to have that old hag moping around here, putting both the girl and me in a bad mood. I talked to Stella about this on one occasion, and naturally Stella asked me why I hadn't discussed it with the old hag herself.

"Why haven't you tried getting her to come at some other time?" she asked, laughing.

I told her it was easier said than done. Money and I had had this arrangement for thirty years: She would come here to clean and tidy the place every Thursday at ten. That I had felt pressured into it in the first place is another matter. I distinctly remember saying to the old hag, "Miss Sørensen, it would suit me better if you were to come on Fridays at two o'clock. Thursdays are no good for me."

And I distinctly recall her replying that she could not come on any day but Thursday. If that did not suit, she was sorry but she could not help me.

The fact that she was a friend of Gerd's sister made it only harder for me to maneuver. She knew I had to treat her civilly, if only to disprove what Gerd's sister, my daughter Alice, and all Gerd's other relatives were starting to say: namely, that I was a "brute." She also knew I would need someone to "do" for me in the new apartment, since neither Alice nor Gerd's sister were prepared to help me any longer. I was completely on my own.

In other words, there is no way, I told Stella. No way any of this can be altered. If I were to strike up a conversation with the old hag for the purpose of changing the time appointed for her regular appearances, she would (1) be mortified and (2) turn nasty and spiteful. It would be something along the lines of: *How do you like that? Grutt wants to change an arrangement that has worked perfectly well for thirty years.*

Here, having been given my chance, I might attempt to plead my case. *But, my dear Miss Sørensen, it has* not *always worked perfectly well for me. You may recall the conversation we had when you started cleaning for me, in which I pointed out that Thursday was not the most convenient day?* But then she would, of course, sniff and, claiming to remember no such thing, assure me that if I was dissatisfied with her work, she could easily find more enjoyable things to do of a Thursday. No point staying on where she wasn't wanted. Whereupon I, having shrunk to a nothing before her eyes, would have no course but to retreat: that was not what I had meant at all, it was only a suggestion. And then, with a (clenching) cheeriness, I would be obliged to add, *I only thought a little change in our routine might perhaps perk us up a little, Miss Sørensen.*

But here we are again, with Money letting herself in just as I am about to get into the bath. I had intended to bathe before the funeral service, which starts at 1 P.M., and then walk to the crematorium, to be sure of arriving on time. I could, of course, lock the bathroom door and call out to her that she needn't clean in here today, since I'm in the bath. But she would take offense at that, too. So now I'll have to get dressed and go out and say good morning—and wouldn't you know, I've left my socks in the living room. I have no choice. I'll have to walk all the way through the apartment to fetch them, sure to bump into her, I in my bare feet.

"Good morning, Miss Sørensen."

In the living room, she turns from the windowsill she has been dusting and looks across at me; her wrinkled old moosh is painted red, her cheeks caked with makeup, the effect altogether hectic. She smiles faintly, a sour smile; she doesn't fool me with her fake warmth. The sour smile turns into a more genuinely sarcastic grin when her eyes fall on my naked feet.

"Good morning, Grutt." She turns back to the window. "Looks like we're going to get some sunshine in September, too."

She is grinning sarcastically at my naked old feet, when I notice a run in the left leg of her panty hose. Not only that, but I happen to have noticed that same run perhaps three weeks ago, indicating that she has not changed her panty hose in weeks, and for all I know months, that old slattern, standing there, with her face turned away, grinning sarcastically.

"My friend Stella is being buried today," I say.

She says nothing.

"I've never been able to make up my mind what sort of weather I feel is right for such occasions," I go on. "I've always associated sunshine with death and rain with life, so as far as I can see it's only right and proper that the sun should be shining today. I hope it shines on my funeral, too."

Money, still standing there, still staring out the window, then says, "I don't know whether I told you, Grutt ... *Axel* ... how truly sorry I am, for your sake, that Stella is gone. And of course I can't help thinking about her girls. I mean, Axel, I've met Amanda here a few times, when she's visited you. ..."

In what gutter did we get onto first-name terms? I want to ask but bite it back. Instead, I mutter, "Well, we all have to go sometime, Miss Sørensen."

I feel like adding that I think it highly—*highly*—inconsiderate of her to bring up Stella's and Amanda's names like that, with me standing here in the middle of the living room barefoot. That's so typical of her.

"Old hag!" I whisper.

She turns and looks at me. "Did you say something, Grutt?"

"I said I'm going to have that bath now," I hiss. Then, grinning sheepishly, I look at her face. She reminds me of my mother—there's the same tightness around the lips—even though she's fifteen years younger than I am and at least twenty years older than my mother lived to be. "I have to take a bath before the funeral," I say.

I grab my socks, which I had left lying on the sofa, debate for a moment whether to put them on, to save leaving the room in my bare feet, but then she would stand there in the light from the window, watching me while I sat down on the sofa and clumsily pulled them on. I couldn't stand that. Pulling on socks is both an intimate and a strenuous task, impossible to accomplish with other people watching. I opt, therefore, for the lesser of two evils and leave the room with as much dignity as can be feigned in my condition.

WHEN I MET STELLA, she had just met Martin, the man to whom she was subject until her death. Her word, not mine: *subject*, she said. Nonsense, I said. If it hadn't been Martin, it would've been someone else. No, she said firmly. *Subject!* I, for my part, am subject to my own aging body: the aching joints, the nervous twitching of the right eye, the constant ringing tone (a high C) in the left ear, the most unpleasant feeling of being forever at the beck and call of nature; though nothing ever comes, I still need to go, an affliction as intolerable as it is ridiculous. Then there is the heart that simply misses a beat every now and again, not that it bothers me, but it is a reminder, nonetheless, of the way things are going. And if that weren't enough, I have a blister on my right foot that makes me limp when I wear my new dress shoes. So I am, in fact, subject to a pair of shoes. And I am subject to the Oslo Municipal Highways Department, which does not sand the sidewalks in the winter; subject to the weather, because in January the streets are like sheets of ice underfoot, and in July I grow faint with the heat, the relentlessly bright light. I am subject to all the hogwash that our newspapers and television channels spew at me, day in, day out, and subject to the appalling musical tastes of my neighbor, even older than I and almost stone-deaf besides. I am subject to my lack of faith in

God and a life hereafter, and to my fear of falling and not dying (death doesn't frighten me), but instead surviving as a helpless, drooling vegetable *subject* to the condescending care of health-care professionals.

But to another person? No, I have never been subject to another person as Stella said she was.

"I don't believe that."
  "What don't you believe?"
  "That you've never been subject to another person in that way."
  "Believe what you like, Stella, but I'm the one who knows."

Martin was a handsome man, just as Stella was a good-looking woman. He *is* a handsome man. I mean, he didn't exactly jump after her when she fell, so as far as that goes he is still among us. The question is whether he tried to save her, or whether he actually pushed her. I know he's been questioned time and again by the police; they must have their suspicions, as I have mine, about so many things. But I do not believe he pushed her. Not deliberately. Husbands are forever being blamed for the misfortunes of their wives, and here I speak from experience. Stella was too good for him; it's as simple as that. In my view he is a conceited ass (and I said as much to the extraordinary policewoman who interviewed me about the case); he is a brute, but he did not kill her. Such things do, after all, take courage of a sort.

Amanda

Everything the minister says in church today is a bunch of lies, because:

1. I don't believe in God. I don't believe in death. I don't believe in Mamma. I don't believe in Pappa.
2. I don't believe in the earth. I don't believe in heaven. I don't believe in the stars. I don't believe in the trees. I don't believe in the grass. I don't believe in the birds.
3. I don't believe in Norway. I don't believe in the prime minister. I don't believe what anybody says.
4. I don't believe in my body, my breasts, my hair, my hands, my eyes, my teeth, or my mouth.

I tell Bee that Mamma falls and falls and never hits the ground. I tell her that Mamma meets a big blue bird, and the bird says loftily, "Falling is not the same as flying."

"Huh!" says Mamma. "What would you know about that?"

"Ah, what indeed?" says the bird, and off he flies.

Soon Mamma meets a squirrel and a cod, and the squirrel and the cod say sadly, "Falling is not the same as flying."

"Huh! What would you two know about that?" says Mamma.

"Ah, what indeed?" say the squirrel and the cod, and they go on falling.

Then Mamma meets an old woman whom God has chucked out of heaven because she was so grumpy and tight-lipped.

"Hello, Mother," says Mamma.

"Hello, Daughter," says the old woman.

"What are you doing here, halfway between heaven and earth?" asks Mamma.

"God chucked me out of heaven because I was so grumpy and tight-lipped," says the old woman. "What are *you* doing here?"

"I fell off a roof, and now I'm just falling and falling without ever hitting the ground," says Mamma.

"Well, you can take it from me, falling is not the same as flying," says the old woman.

"Huh! What would you know about that?" says Mamma.

"Ah, what indeed?" says the old woman, and she goes on falling.

Axel

It was a green sofa that brought them together. Stella was living alone with her daughter, Amanda. An aunt had left her some money, and with this money she decided to buy a sofa. Martin worked for an exclusive furniture store in Oslo; it was his job to deliver goods to customers' homes. That was how they met. If I had been in Stella's shoes I would have spent the money on other things—music or wine, or, had I been younger, a trip to London to try out the new Ferris wheel there, the London Eye. But Stella spent her money on a green sofa. It so happens that I have sat on that sofa. It was not to my taste at all, a long hard modern piece of furniture that resembled nothing so much as a tight green female mouth.

Stella told me that, having delivered the sofa, Martin did not want to leave. He had had himself and the sofa hoisted up the outside of the building to the apartment in which she lived, and they materialized right outside her window on the ninth floor.

"All at once he was just there, sitting on the sofa, handsome, smiling, outside my window."

I remember how she sat on the edge of my bed and laughed when she told me.

"I asked him to leave, but he wouldn't. He refused. And then . . . well, then he moved in."

. . .

I can imagine how Stella, on catching sight of Martin outside her window, must have seen her own face reflected in his. The same narrow blue eyes, the same full lower lip, the same large hooked nose. They were both skinny and thin-skinned, every single muscle, every bone on display. Sometimes those two faces reminded me of another face, the face of a man I had once known slightly. Rolf Larsen was his name. He ended up in Dachau during the war. He survived, after a fashion, and when I met him again, quite by chance, on Karl Johans Gate in Oslo, it was that thin-skinned face that shocked me most. His words as to where he had been and what they had done went in one ear and out the other. The skin around his eyes, mouth, and cheekbones was too tight, pulled taut. It could have ripped open at any moment to reveal—what?—a gaping mouth? A scream?

Eventually, such faces were to be seen everywhere. You could hardly open a newspaper without coming across pictures of them, the faces of war, and these days I hardly even notice them. But on those few occasions that I saw Stella and Martin together, I remembered Rolf Larsen. I never thought of it when Stella was alone. Her face was always changing, or evolving, as if it could not decide what sort of face it ought to be and so reflected the facial features of whomever she was with—which is not to say that she grew old and wrinkled when she was with me. The transformation was more subtle than that.

She herself used to say, "Martin is a more beautiful version of me." Naturally, she was deaf to my vehement protests. Stella hated her own reflection. One time at my apartment, on her way back from the bathroom to the living room, she stopped in front of the gilt mirror in the hall. She did not know that I could see her from the living room. (In fact she never knew how I hung on her every word, followed her every move, when she visited me.) She stopped in front of the mirror and leaned forward, peering at her own reflection—and then she made a face so horrible I almost dropped my coffee cup. She dug her nails into her cheeks and clawed and clawed at herself, the way a child, unhappy with a drawing, will scribble over the whole thing in a temper. Then she straightened up, ran a hand through her hair, moistened her lips with her tongue, and returned to the living room—to me— as if nothing had happened: gleeful, almost, with two red spots on her cheeks.

Not long after Martin moved in with her, as he promptly did, he asked Stella to come with him to Høylandet to meet his family. His grandmother—his father's mother, that is—was soon to turn seventy-five, an event that was to be celebrated in grand style. I was still in the hospital. Stella was glowing when she came into my room and sat down on my bed.

"He wants to take me way out into the middle of nowhere, by plane and train and bus and God knows what else. Me, who's so scared of flying!"

I looked at her, puzzled. "*He?* He who?" I asked, trying to be patient.

"Martin!" she cried, rolling her eyes. "He wants to take me home . . . to the farm . . . to meet his family: mother, father, ostriches, the lot."

"Ostriches?"

"His parents have an ostrich farm," she explained. "It's an experiment. His dad has been given a government permit. He thinks ostriches are going to be the farming sensation of the nineties or something. But listen! His grandmother Harriet is turning seventy-five. We're going to a birthday party!"

I turned away, muttering a few choice sarcastic remarks about Middle Norway, birthdays, and grandmothers. But hadn't they, I wondered, only known each other a few weeks? Well, yes, she said, that was true, but he had already moved in with her, so surely there was nothing to keep them from going away together. She gave me a look, imploring or anxious—as if it mattered whether I gave her my blessing.

"So when do you leave?"

"Tomorrow."

"How long will you be away?"

"Four days, maybe five."

"But aren't you on duty?"

"I can swap shifts with one of the others."

All I could think was that if she left the next day I would never see her again. I was due to be discharged in three days, due in three days to return to my miserable old-man's existence. The thought of never seeing her again made me do an odd thing; ten years later I still cringe with embarrassment. I don't know what came over me—I don't like outbursts of any kind and prefer not to be the butt of other people's sentimentality. Being touched by other people upsets me; I actually find it physically unpleasant, and I instinctively pull away when I sense an imminent embrace or a caress. Because the last thing I want to do is to hurt anyone, I usually feign a sneeze or a violent fit of coughing so the person closing in on me will not think I am spurning the advance. (Of course my wife, Gerd, was not fooled. How many times did I cough in her face as we lay side by side in our narrow marriage bed; how many times did she turn away with cold, wounded eyes, reproaching me with her naked, slightly coarse back, which I could never bring myself to stroke or put an arm around?) But when I realized I was never going to see Stella again, I touched her. I was sitting up in my bed, she was perched on its edge, and suddenly I grabbed her right hand and pressed it against my cheek. (She had such a slender supple wrist, no sharp rings or jangling bracelets, just warm skin.) And she did not take her hand away—even after I let go of it. She stayed where she was, very still, very close.

Then something burst out of me: words . . . gibberish . . . sobs . . . I don't know what all. I vomited, too, as if all the nastiness inside me was being forced up my gullet and out. And then I let out something like a howl.

"Hush now, Axel, hush," she whispered. "It's going to be okay, it'll be okay." She spoke to me the way a mother speaks to her child, comforting it. "Hush now, Axel, hush."

It had been ages since anyone had called me Axel. I bowed my head. In gratitude. With Stella's hand on my cheek.

Then she said, "We're going to be friends, you and I. This isn't the last time; you know that, don't you? I can come to see you at your apartment, and we'll have our chats, and we'll have coffee. I want you to meet my daughter—you know, Amanda?— she'll be five next week. And I want you to meet Martin."

I felt a twinge of uneasiness. It might have been better to say goodbye there and then. There's no denying that I looked forward to seeing Stella at the hospital, but that she should show up at my apartment, that she and I should sit on my gray sofa drinking coffee and chatting, seemed at that moment completely unlikely. In my mind the difficulties multiplied. Would I have to serve something with the coffee? What would we talk about? She was only twenty-five at the time. What did one say to a twenty-five-year-old? What would Money say? Maybe I was just a pathetic old man. I had never had many close friends; there had only been Isak Skald, really, and over the years he and I had developed a set of unwritten rules to govern our friendship. He called me Grutt, for example, and I called him Skald. It's not that we were especially formal or polite with each other, this was simply what we did. We were careful when we discussed personal matters. Since he was my doctor, it was only natural for me to tell him about my physical ailments; and just as naturally, he responded by offering medical advice. But to save our friendship from being confused with a straightforward doctor-patient relationship, he informed me of *his* physical ailments, too. Since we both suffered from an enlarged prostate, this was an obvious topic of conversation. Occasionally we would talk about his wife, Else, that marvelous woman with the hands that could change a man's life, but all in all I would say that we talked more about our prostates. And I don't think we ever mentioned my Gerd.

Skald had heard that Stella and I were having these daily bedside chats, that she sometimes brought her lunch to my room instead of eating with her colleagues. Was it possible, he wondered, that I was infatuated with this young woman? I made it clear that I found such insinuations offensive. If Stella were to have coffee with me at my apartment, this was exactly the sort of comment I was worried about. When you got right down to it, there was no good reason for Stella and me to see each other. I had nothing to offer. I felt vaguely shy when she was around, and it bothered me. Shy and ashamed, even. As if I were seeing myself, my face and my body, with her eyes. These clumsy hands of mine with their stiff fingers, not nimble enough.

Once Stella and I were having a snack in my room. She kept fingering the silver locket that hung on a chain around her neck. It had been her mother's. Finally the clasp came undone and the locket slid to the floor. Stella dropped onto all fours.

"Dammit," she muttered, "dammit, I can't see it." But, after groping around for a while: "Here it is! Found it! Under the bed!" She stood up, hair a mess, a big smile on her face. "Got it!"

She brushed off her uniform and handed me the silver locket. It was so tiny in my hand. I looked at it lying there, glinting on my palm, and thought what an insult it was for something so small and silvery and feminine to be put into an ancient paw like mine. She sat on the edge of the bed with her back to me, gathered up her long hair, and bent her head, baring her long white neck. I looked away.

"The clasp is so tricky. Could you fasten it for me?"

I looked at the necklace between my fingers. I looked at the nape of her neck. I looked at my hands.

"I'm not very good with itty-bitty things like this." I tried a little laugh.

"Sure you are, it's easy," she said. "It's only hard to fasten if you're the one wearing it."

Face turned away, hair gathered up, she told me how this particular clasp worked. I looked at the nape of her neck and caught a faint whiff of perspiration and of something else I couldn't put my finger on, a not unpleasant but rather spicy odor that always seemed to cling to Stella. Gently I laid the chain around her neck, my hands trembling, all the cuff links I was no longer capable of clipping to my shirtsleeves flashing through my mind.

"Can't you manage it?" she asked.

"Now, now, be patient, Stella," I whispered.

I eventually got the catch open. Then all I had to do was to hook it through a little loop in the chain and—*click*—that would be that. But even my good eye let me down—well, it would, wouldn't it, watering, misting over—and my hands trembled even more.

In the end I completely botched it, and the locket slid down into her lap. She turned and smiled at me. I looked down.

"Just a minute," she chirped, getting to her feet. "I'll see if Lena's down the hall, I can ask her to do it. Trust Mamma to leave me a necklace with such a tricky clasp. She probably thought I'd never be able to take it off and would have to keep it round my neck forever."

She winked at me.

I nodded as she went out the door.

I curled my fingers in like claws.

"Butterfingers!" I hissed at my hands.

I bit off a chunk of bread. Chewed and chewed, but couldn't seem to swallow.

Amanda

After the funeral, Martin the ostrich king will take Bee by the hand and bring her home. Martin isn't my father. My father's in Australia. Martin is Bee's father; that's why it's up to him to take Bee by the hand and bring her back here. Bee will sleep in this room and wake up in this room, but Mamma won't be here, and I won't be here, and the plumber won't be here.

Once, when Bee was just a baby, the ostrich king and I went to Copenhagen for my birthday. He had promised me a ride on the Ferris wheel. The old geezer told me that if it hadn't been for his great-uncle in America, there wouldn't be any Ferris wheels, and without Ferris wheels, the old geezer said, the world would have been a poorer place. Who knows? The old geezer says a lot of weird things. But it didn't come to anything, that Ferris wheel ride. Instead, the ostrich king and I went on the roller coaster, up and down and up and down. Now I'm not afraid of anything; back then, though, I was afraid. The ostrich king just laughed at me and we did it again. Afterward we went back to the hotel room, and I lay on my bed and watched TV, and the ostrich king lay on his bed and slept. The curtains were drawn.

On my birthday I ordered hot dogs, French fries, and a soda from room service.

The ostrich king slept for three days. He said he'd never slept so well. Dreamless.

Then we headed home again.

Axel

A bath before the funeral. Attending to one's toilet becomes an increasingly arduous task as one ages. But as long as I have plenty of time, and as long as neither impatience nor fear gets the better of me, I can, nonetheless, make myself presentable.

Some years ago I took one of my last trips abroad, to Arezzo in Italy. There was an archaeologist there, Paolo, or Massimo; I don't recall his name. But I do remember being invited into his workshop, where I saw all the fragments of stone jars on which he was working. To me this collection looked like a bunch of old rocks, but he was proud of them because they were old, thousands of years old. And if you put them together in the right way, said Paolo or Massimo, if you understood how this stone fit with that, then you would also understand something very important about something-or-other—I've forgotten what. It wasn't the thought of some grand design that impressed me, however, it was the way the archaeologist worked. He handled each fragment with precision, gentleness, care, and deliberation, always in the knowledge that it could crack, crumble away, turn to dust. It was a beautiful sight: the archaeologist's fingers, the remarkable rapport between hand and eye.

Sometimes I feel about my body much as the archaeologist seemed to feel about his stones. It's as though my body is a heap of rocks that has to be made presentable, put on display, possibly commented on (Well, how about that? Don't tell me he's still alive!). I should not have to feel ashamed of my appearance were it not for the fear that this body, this load of old rocks, might let me down. Because it is constantly threatening to humiliate me, belittle me, make me look foolish.

There is fear. I am still afraid.

The archaeologist said nothing about fear. Those stones were not his body. He said the stones were his life, but they were not his body. There is a difference. Before I left him in his workshop, he gave me a stone and asked me to take good care of it because it was very old, probably at least 2,300 years old. And I took this 2,300-year-old stone home and set it on my bedside table, in an ashtray, under the lamp. I would gaze at it respectfully every night before getting into bed. I would think warmly of the archaeologist in his workshop. I would try to imagine where that stone had been, all the centuries to which it could bear witness, were it a living being and not a stone; but a stone it was, and a stone it remained, and as such it could not bear witness to anything at all.

Then it happened. One evening about three weeks after my return from Italy, the stone was gone. The stone was gone, the ashtray washed and put back in the kitchen closet. Old hag! I thought. Obviously Money had thrown out what she took to be a piece of junk, a worthless hunk of rock.

She always has to ruin things for me.

I realized that there was no point in bringing the matter up with her; she would just stare blankly at me, take offense. I mean, what does she know of 2,300-year-old stones or grand designs? For my own part, I felt bad about the archaeologist. The thought of him kept me awake several nights running. Not that there's anything unusual about that, but this time all I could think about was the lost stone, the archaeologist's hands, his fingers, the look in his eyes, ancient treasures of great moment. It seemed to me that I had been careless enough to lose a tiny fragment of life itself—not my own life, you understand, but the archaeologist's. He must have felt it, the loss of the stone—the stone he had given me, entrusted to me—he must have felt the loss like a physical pain.

In the end, I was so consumed with guilt that I looked up the archaeologist's telephone number in Italy and called him. In my decent English I explained to the somewhat bewildered gentleman who answered the phone that I had done my best to look after the 2,300-year-old stone, but that an old hag had thrown it away, probably down the garbage chute outside my apartment.

There was a long silence on the other end of the line. And then the man said, "Ahhh!"

"Yes?" I said, anxiously.

"It is all right!" he said. "Not to worry!"

"Not to worry?" I whispered.

"No," he replied, "not to worry!"

"No?"

"No!"

Then he said "Ciao!" and hung up.

I've been cut open, had my insides reorganized, and been sewn up again any number of times. And it has hurt. Even my heart has been slit open and handled. There is nothing more to be got from my body. It cannot be cut open and sewn up again. I have nothing more to give. Before, my fear was abstract, hypothetical, diffuse. I was subject to frequent bouts of melancholy, which suited me fine. With Gerd I could always blame things on my melancholy, thus securing dispensation to do as I pleased: an agreeable arrangement. Now my fear is concrete and prosaic. Take this business of the bath, for example. I have managed to ease my old carcass into the bath without falling over, but I still have to get out again, which means I cannot enjoy the hot water for wondering how that is to be done. I am afraid I will slip on the bathroom floor and crack my head against the edge of the tub. I am afraid I will pass out here, overcome by the heat; afraid of being found by Money, unconscious, naked, helpless; afraid of not being found at all, of turning into a stinking corpse for the neighbors to discuss in horrified whispers; afraid of ending up as an item in the newspaper: "Naked old man slips on bathroom floor, lies dead for a week before police break down door." (What would my daughter say? Would she bow her head for a moment and think back on us two, Dad and Alice, and all the times she came running to meet me, arms outstretched? Or would she quickly, quietly, and efficiently organize funeral and wreath, soon to return, tight-lipped, to her quick, quiet, and efficient life as a middle-aged woman with a husband, two grown-up children, and her first grandchild on the way?)

In my former life, I liked to go swimming, liked to feel the water loosening up muscles, skin, joints. In my former life, I liked a lot of things without really appreciating them. I liked to eat good food. These days I can no longer taste the difference between a slice of coarse whole wheat and a slice of soft white bread. I used to like fine wines. These days it makes no difference whether it is a Bordeaux or an American cabernet. Every once in a while, I still treat myself to some good food and fine wine, but the joy is gone.

Amanda

Things I believe in:

1. I believe in Snip, Snap, and Snout. I believe in their fingers running through my hair, which just gets longer and longer. I believe in thirty fingers running through my hair, six hands stroking my body, three mouths kissing mine.
2. I believe that I might catch fire at any minute.

But I don't say things like that to Bee. She's just a little girl. She doesn't even have breasts yet.

Axel

Yes, the joy is gone.

I used to take joy in the lazy turn of a Ferris wheel, so beautifully constructed, so brilliantly conceived. I once told Amanda about the engineer George Washington Ferris, the inventor of the Ferris wheel, and my relative. Martha Ferris, the engineer's mother, was my father's second cousin. When I was a boy, my father took me for a ride on a Ferris wheel, not a particularly big one but breathtaking all the same. When we reached the top he looked down and said, "You know, you could stand up, stretch out your arms, and jump. That's what hits me up here. You could actually do it!"

I told Amanda that George Washington Ferris built his fabulous wheel for the World's Columbian Exposition in Chicago in 1893, in no small part to impress his charming wife, Margaret Ann. This wheel, which was 250 feet in diameter, cost $400,000 to construct. It was to be the biggest wheel ever, the most magnificent mechanical invention of all time. The axle—the very heart of the wheel, Amanda!—weighed sixty-three tons, the largest iron part ever to be cast in one piece, and around this axle 1,440 passengers could ride at a time, up into the air and down again, up into the air and down, up into the air and down.

Stella Descending

On June 17, 1893, Ferris's charming wife raised her champagne glass to toast her husband. She was sitting, at the time, at the top of the wheel, from which point she could see the whole of Chicago. Her voice was soft. *To the health of my husband and the success of the Ferris wheel.*

"She drank a toast," I told Amanda, "to her husband and his wonderful invention. Because strictly speaking, you see, that is its correct name: the Ferris wheel, which is what Americans call it, and not the Parisian wheel, as it is known in Europe, or the Big Wheel, as the British call it. He was greater than Gustave Eiffel, Amanda, and yet no one now remembers him at all."

"But was his wife happy that he had made a wheel for her?"

"I don't think she ever set foot on a Ferris wheel again," I said. "She left him three years later. He was all washed up. He owed money right, left, and center. The fabulous wheel had cost too much to build, and people gradually lost interest. George Washington Ferris was told to knock the thing down, but when he tried to sell it for scrap, no one would buy it. Some people say the Germans eventually took it off his hands and later used it to make guns during the First World War."

"And what happened to the inventor? What happened to Ferris?"

"He died. Of a broken heart, it was said. His charming wife, the magnificent wheel—scrap, the lot of it. The joy was gone."

Amanda reminds me that once, a long time ago, I took pleasure in teaching. As a young man I dreamed of making a difference as a teacher. I even used such words as *inspiration, bequeathing,* and ... well ... *joy.* But I never did hit it off with my fellow teachers. The older ones could not forgive my so-called treachery during the war. The younger ones ignored me. And the students ... I never managed to get through to them. They wouldn't listen to me. In the end I gave up, grew sardonic and baleful. Alienated them. Earned myself the nickname Gruesome Grutt.

"Why didn't they like you, Axel? What did they blame you for? What happened during the war?"

Stella stands before the gilt mirror in the hall, looking at me.

"Come on, Axel, tell me. I tell you everything, don't I?"

A few days ago, I read a newspaper article in which some old people answered the question: Given the chance, would you live your life over again? Most of them said yes. How could they? How could anyone live his life again? Go through all that toil and trouble again? It's only fair to point out that the reporter had not set out to describe the lot of the elderly in Norway. This was one of those so-called feel-good pieces, human-interest stuff, aimed at younger people who are working themselves to death and not taking time to enjoy the important things in life: their children, their family, and so on. (I've never understood how one is supposed to *enjoy* one's family. I was certainly never able to *enjoy* mine.) These elderly interviewees figured merely as cautionary waxworks of a sort, a grim reminder of what lies ahead. *Enjoy life while you've still got it!* That was how the journalist concluded his article. Enjoy life? Live it over again? Never! These days I'm most afraid that I'm going to end up living forever, unless I take matters into my own hands; afraid that God, if he exists, has forgotten all about me; that Death, busy as life is, has forgotten me, too.

Having had my bath and hoisted myself out of the tub, I plant myself squarely in front of the mirror. Swathed in a yellow bathrobe, I shave—and my hand is steady. It does not tremble. It does its work with precision, gentleness, care, and deliberation. When I finish shaving, I will get dressed. I laid my clothes out last night. I shall wear dark blue slacks, a dark blue jacket, a white shirt I ironed five days ago, the same day I heard of her death, and a blue tie. I do not need a walking stick. I have a good firm step for my age. I have a green felt hat to which I am greatly attached.

.   .   .

I suppose I do have one joy; there is pleasure for me in music. I have never played an instrument, and I only ever sing to myself, very quietly, under the eiderdown at night. I used to sing at the moment when the Ferris wheel gondola reached its highest point: I would stand up, stretch out my arms, and sing. Music tells me there are beings beyond this miserable existence who are willing to speak to us. Unborn children, perhaps, who were meant to have a body, a voice, a life, but who came to nothing, aborted or snuffed out at the moment of conception, and turned instead into music that some composer was sensitive enough to catch and write down.

I know there are other sorts of reality. I can hear them there, on the other side, a bequest from the outermost limits.

Mind you, my neighbor does his best to spoil it for me. I've lost count of the times over the years I've had to bang on the wall because he's put on the racket he calls music. And the old boy's nearly stone-deaf. One morning I rang his doorbell and tried, as politely as I know how, to persuade him to buy a hearing aid like mine, with headphones and none of those fiddly little screws or knobs. But the old fool took my overture as an insult.

For one thing, he said, there was nothing wrong with his hearing. And for another, he had no problem adjusting his hearing aid.

Naturally I had to ask him why he had a hearing aid, if there was nothing wrong with his hearing. That was when he slammed the door in my face.

"Well, thank *you*!" I yelled.

I heard him behind the door, muttering something under his breath. Then he shuffled off to what I presumed to be a very expensive modern stereo system and turned the volume up even louder. Some second-rate opera singer, I think it was, screeching her way through a frightful libretto that someone had slapped onto a clarinet concerto by Mozart.

That did it. I marched back to my own apartment and turned up the volume on my own stereo. I have a CD of Janet Baker singing Mahler so divinely anyone would think Mahler had written the piece with her in mind. I shut my eyes.

I opened my eyes. My neighbor had turned his racket up even louder—in order to drown out my Mahler.

I hammered on the wall.

My neighbor hammered on his wall.

I turned up the volume.

My neighbor turned up his volume.

The whole building rang with the noise.

Every now and then, time seems to pass without my being aware of it. I get confused. The day starts and the day ends, and all of a sudden it's nighttime. Where have I been? What have I done?

I heard the sound of running feet and voices on the stairs. Loud knocking on my door. A man's voice shouting, "Grutt! Grutt! Are you okay?"

I stepped out into the hall, past the gilt mirror, and calmly opened the door.

"Are you okay?" asked the young dark-haired man standing outside. He was panting for breath. I recognized him. He lived two floors above me; as far as I knew he was a writer and a conceited ass. It was difficult to hear what he was saying. Mahler was drowning everything out.

"Why, yes, I'm perfectly okay," I replied.

I did my best to speak in a normal voice, even though the music was so loud. By now I could hear only my music. My neighbor must have switched his off.

"But you're waking the whole building," the young man shouted, looking over my shoulder as if expecting to see women dancing languorously around my living room.

"It's Mahler!" I shouted.

"Right, but this just isn't okay."

I looked at him, wanting to explain that I knew very well the music was far too loud. Everything went quiet for a moment, long enough for us both to catch our breath. We eyed each other. A few seconds passed. Then the music struck up again from the first track on the CD. I jumped.

"It's Mahler," I repeated, gazing at the floor. "My neighbor was mangling Mozart; it was unbearable. You must have heard it. I know I shouldn't play it so loud. I beg your pardon. But he was mangling Mozart. . . . Won't you come in? I'll turn down the volume and you can listen to it yourself—to Mahler, I mean."

The young man sighed, glanced at his watch.

"It's past two o'clock," he said. "I went to bed hours ago: me, my wife, our kids, and the dog. The whole gang. It's the middle of the night, don't you realize that? And it just keeps playing over and over. Did you forget to cancel the repeat button?"

"No . . . yes . . . I've—I don't know."

Now I was confused. I said, "Couldn't you come in for a moment, so we can sort this out?"

The young man glanced at his watch again, suddenly at a loss.

"I want you to hear Mahler as he ought to be heard," I went on, firmly now. "That's Janet Baker singing—anyone would think Mahler wrote this with her in mind. . . . Listen! It's all about a child dying—his own, you understand. His own child."

The young man shrugged, as if about to turn and go, but to my astonishment he followed me into the living room and sat down on the sofa. I turned the sound down. Janet Baker's divine voice filled the room.

"Well, maybe we could sit here for a little while," the young man said, "and listen to your music. Without having to talk to each other, and without having to do it again another night out of sheer politeness."

"Right," I said.

And so we sat there in my living room, listening to Mahler, this conceited young ass and me. He probably wasn't all that bad once you got to know him—which I, of course, never did because we never did it again. We nodded politely when we bumped into each other on the stairs, but we never did it again—and then, a few months ago, he moved out, leaving behind his wife, his children, and the dog. I don't know where he went. We did not say goodbye.

Since then it has occurred to me that I should possibly have played Schubert instead. It doesn't do to be too stirred up when you listen to Mahler. Schubert might have given him more joy . . . or solace. Sometimes when I say joy, I mean solace.

Amanda

"Shut your eyes, Bee," I say.

"They are shut," says Bee.

"When you're alone with the ostrich king, you have to imagine that Mamma is close by. Not right here, but close by."

"Okay," says Bee. "But she's dead, really, isn't she?"

"Yes," I say. "That's right."

Bee looks at the ceiling.

"But that doesn't mean she's not close by," I say. "When you're alone, you have to imagine that her arms are long, thousands of times longer than wings, thousands of times longer than my hair and your hair; her arms are so long that she can reach out any time, take you by the hand, and lead you away."

Axel

When she came back from the trip to Høylandet she was different. I don't know whether this change was due to the new surroundings—my apartment, instead of the sterile hospital room to which we had both grown accustomed—or whether it was something else, something that was, to me, intangible, unmanageable. More than once I came close to canceling our coffee klatch. The night before, I couldn't sleep and my stomach ached. In the morning, after I had bathed and dressed, I walked down to the corner store, picked up freshly ground coffee and milk, and bought a layer cake from the patisserie. I decked the coffee table with candles, a cloth, and china. I tidied up and vacuumed, plumped the cushions, and folded the red plaid rug.

Ten minutes before she was supposed to arrive, I sank into a chair and burst into tears.

She rang the bell at one o'clock on the dot. It was a glorious, sunny, frozen Saturday in February. The first thing that struck me was that I had to raise my head to look her in the eye. She towered over me. Up to that point our relationship had been defined by the fact that I lay propped up in a hospital bed, tucked into a nest of white pillows and quilts, while she sat on the edge in her white uniform. Now she was wearing a yellow polo-neck sweater and a long black skirt. Her cheeks were apricot-pink and wet with tears from the winter wind, her eyes sparkling, her long fair hair caught up in a loose knot. She laid her hands on my shoulders and planted a kiss on my brow.

"I brought some fresh rolls." She smiled. "Baked them myself!"

I pulled away from her and muttered something about making the coffee. Back in the kitchen, I stared numbly at the layer cake I had set out on a dish, ready to serve. I almost started to cry again. She was bound to think it ridiculous, over the top; she had brought fresh-baked rolls, clearly far more appropriate for a simple cup of coffee. Layer cake indeed! It was hardly as if anyone was celebrating a birthday! Hardly as if there was anything to celebrate at all. To serve a layer cake would be to give her the idea that I expected a great deal of this visit. It would put far too much pressure on an already strained situation. So I opened the cabinet under the sink, grabbed the serving dish, and tipped the cake into the garbage. I was licking the icing off my fingers when she appeared at my back.

"What a lovely apartment, Axel."

She looked at me, looked at the empty cake dish, looked at the open door, the cabinet under the sink. "Don't tell me you've been baking!" She laughed.

I shook my head.

"You've got some icing on your cheek." Still smiling, she ran her right index finger across my cheek and popped her finger into her mouth.

"Mmmm," she said, and winked. "Vanilla icing. . . . Have you got something up your sleeve?"

"No, not at all!" I said. "I had people over for dinner yesterday, and one of the ladies brought a cake. I was rude enough to eat the last slice before you got here. Well, I didn't want to offer you the remains of last night's cake. But Stella, why don't you sit yourself down in the living room. I'll put your rolls onto a dish, organize some bread and cheese, and make the coffee."

"I'll give you a hand," she said.

"Stella, go sit down! Please! I'll see to this."

I was close to tears again. She smiled hesitantly and left me to myself in the kitchen, giving me a chance to dry my eyes and shove the ill-fated layer cake deeper in the garbage can. Then I put on the coffee.

The next hour passed uneventfully. We sat on the sofa, ate fresh-baked rolls, and drank coffee. She talked. She smelled sweet. She laughed. I didn't say much; I didn't need to. She was full of all the things she had seen and done on her short trip to central Norway with her new boyfriend.

"We left early Friday morning," Stella said. "Flew from Fornebu to Værnes. We could have flown to Namsos, which is closer, but it would have cost a lot more. He paid for every-thing—"

"I should hope so," I interrupted.

"You can talk," she said, "but we're both pretty strapped for cash. I thought it was really nice of him. Next time it'll be on me. But that's not the point. That's not what I was going to tell you. The thing is, Axel, I've always been so afraid of flying. It's not natural for human beings to fly; we belong on the ground. It's not natural to put yourself so unconditionally and so helplessly into the hands of another human being—the captain, I mean. That he should have to carry so many bodies up into the air at one time, fly from one town to another, one country to another, goes against everything—the force of gravity, the survival instinct, the need for control, the amount of faith that I, for one, am able to put in others. How do I know that all the people who had a hand in building that particular plane were one hundred percent on the ball and knew what they were doing? Who's to say there wasn't some nutcase among them? And how do I know that the mechanics, the guys whose job it is to check that every-thing's in working order, weren't a bit hung over the day I hap-pened to be flying out and cut a few corners? And how do I know that the captain didn't find his darling in the arms of another man the night before? What if he decides the best revenge would be to send himself and everyone else on board plummeting to their deaths?"

"You just have to trust people," I ventured.

"So says Axel Grutt, who's never trusted a living soul."

I mumbled something or other, but she carried on.

"Anyway, that's the reason I don't fly very often—that and lack of cash, of course. But Martin tried to help me. He knows I can't resist a challenge. Just last week he said he would cook me the most wonderful seven-course dinner if I would dress as a man—his clothes, fake mustache, hat, coat, the lot—and go down to the supermarket with him. Well, on the way to the airport he said, 'Stella, if you can manage to fly from Fornebu to Værnes without panicking, I'll give you an ostrich egg.' I laughed and asked what good an ostrich egg was going to be to me when the plane crashed and we were catapulted into nothingness.

"It went on like that. You know, of course—you do know, don't you, Axel?—that I didn't want him to see how afraid I was. He seems so sure of himself, and I feel so awkward and afraid when I'm with him. I'm never afraid with you, Axel, but with him . . . anyway, I got on the plane and squeezed my eyes tight shut. I didn't sleep, but all the same I had a dream. It happens sometimes. I dreamt I was standing in line on the steps up to the high diving platform at Frogner Baths, the ten-meter one, you know? I was standing behind a whole bunch of naked women, all waiting to go off. And every time the signal sounded—this loud shrill trumpet blast—someone would dive. But there was no water in the pool, and everyone who went off was smashed to bits on the bottom. I knew this, knew it all along, we all knew, and yet we stood there on the steps, each waiting her turn . . . and I watched one woman after another stretch out, push off, and dive. It was a dream, right? But I wasn't sleeping. I was sitting in my seat on the plane, next to Martin, with my eyes tight shut, almost overwhelmed by these images, and I couldn't block them out. But I was not sleeping."

Stella fell silent for a moment. Her frankness disconcerted me. But I listened. I did not interrupt.

"But that's not really what I was going to tell you," she went on. "What I was going to tell you was that when my turn came to dive from the platform, just as I drew my breath to push off, the plane actually took a dive for real. It felt as if we had heeled over and dropped straight down. All the passengers screamed— I screamed—but Martin grabbed hold of me and whispered, 'It's okay, Stella, it's okay, I've got you,' and of course it was okay. Well, I'm here, aren't I? Safe and sound, and probably pregnant. It was only a little turbulence. We weren't in any real danger. But I wonder whether that was the minute I stopped being afraid of flying. Forever. All my life I've been afraid, Axel. Afraid of all the terrible things that could happen."

"And now you're not afraid of anything?" I asked, with a hint of irony in my voice.

"No, no," she replied, "of course I am."

"Did my ears deceive me, or did you say you were pregnant?" I said.

She nodded.

"That was quick. How long have you known him, a month?"

"Five weeks and a couple of days," she said. "I don't know for sure that I'm pregnant. I just think I am. I knew the moment Amanda was conceived. Even though that man—Amanda's father—meant nothing to me. I never want to talk about him! I don't ever want to talk about Amanda's father."

"No, heaven forbid," I said. "As far as I'm concerned, you don't have to talk about any of your lovers. In fact, I'd rather you didn't."

"Oh, I'm babbling on again—I know."

"Yes, you are."

"It's just that I wanted you to know about the baby. I can't be sure . . . but I don't think I'm mistaken. I know it happened that night."

"I see."

"It was a cold, white, starlit night, and we were on our way home from the birthday party. It was pretty late, three o'clock, maybe three-thirty, and we had a half-hour walk in the cold night air ahead of us. It had been snowing; the countryside around us was white and still; we were goofing around like a couple of kids, making tracks and snow angels; he stole my hat and threw it up into a fir tree and it got stuck on a branch—and then we came to a lake that had frozen over. We had seen children skating on it earlier in the day, but now all was quiet . . . all was quiet until we heard a faint rumbling far off, coming closer, until suddenly we caught sight of some huge shadows among the trees: massive, weird-looking creatures, heading toward the frozen lake. Martin and I stood perfectly still. Out on the ice the dark shadows began to gather speed; in fact, before we knew it they had broken into a gallop, one after the other. There were a whole lot of them and they didn't lose their balance, they didn't slip, they just went on galloping. For a moment I thought they were some sort of strange prehistoric horse, but as my eyes adjusted to the distance and the darkness I saw that they had feathers, and then I thought of a fairy tale my father used to tell me when I was a little girl, about a golden bird and about the wind rushing and sighing through the trees, and all at once it dawned on me that those weren't horses I saw out there on the ice but ostriches. Ostriches galloping across the ice in the dark of night. 'They've run away from the farm,' Martin whispered. 'They think they're back on the savannah. We have to do something. I'd better call someone.' So he called someone, and after a while a big truck drove up, and Martin's mother and father and three other men jumped out without a sound, and they all started running down to the frozen lake, brandishing torches. By this time the ostriches were standing quite still, all huddled together; they had abruptly come to a halt, as if frozen solid in the winter night. We left then, went home."

Stella looked at me and gave me the ghost of a smile.

"His family breeds ostriches," she explained. "Kind of goes against all the laws of nature, don't you think, keeping giant African birds in the middle of Norway? It made me think. They're tied to the ground—grounded—too big to fly home, to fly at all. Their feathers and wings are absolutely useless."

She fell silent for a moment, looked away.

"That night Martin took my hand in his and said, 'If we have a child now, and if it's a girl, we'll call her Bea after my Swedish great-grandmother, Beatrice. She was the first woman in Scandinavia to have a hat trimmed with ostrich feathers in her wardrobe.'"

Yes, I could tell right away. When she came back from that trip with Martin, she was different. Something had happened. He had touched her, held her, kissed her, opened her up . . . I don't know, I never really knew, had no way of knowing. She didn't say anything; she didn't need to. I could tell by her cheeks, her eyes, her provocative smile.

When she left, on that Saturday afternoon, I made up my mind that I would never see her again.

Well, what did I, an old man—because even back then I was an old man—have to offer a young woman in love? And what did she have to offer me?

Well, there you are, Axel Grutt. What did I have to offer you? What did I have to offer you except visions of your daughter as a young woman—or of your wife, Gerd, as a young woman? Oh, yes, because it was Gerd you were thinking about, wasn't it, ten years ago when I sat there on your sofa that time, flushed and happy and pregnant? And it's Gerd you're thinking about today, isn't it, now that I too am about to return to dust?

Maybe it was that yellow sweater. Gerd had a yellow sweater she wore when she went skiing. Gerd was the athletic type. I, on the other hand, loathe all forms of sporting activity. Or was it that provocative smile or her way of sitting, long legs stretched out, head up, a hand run through her hair. Stella's visit reminded me of the night Gerd came home long after dinnertime, flopped down into a chair, and said, "Now listen to me, Axel, because this is going to hurt!" This was just after the war, and life at work was hellish. I was worn out and, to cap it off, I had had to make my own dinner, since my wife obviously had other things to do that day.

"Well, and what exactly is going to hurt, Gerd?" I asked.

I knew, of course, what it would be. Yet again, it would be something to do with Victor, everybody's golden-haired hero of the Resistance and *my* fellow teacher. She would not give him up. Everyone knew about it. Everyone in the staff room. Every one of those people with whom I normally took my coffee. I don't know whom they pitied more, Axel Grutt the coward, who was being openly cuckolded, or his lovely wife, who was unfortunate enough to be married to him.

Gerd wanted to take Alice, who was nine at the time, away with her and move up north with this other man. There seemed to be no end to Victor's heroic exploits, and now he wanted to take my wife and my child—I take it she *is* my child, I yelled at Gerd—to Tromsø, there to continue the victory celebrations. Nothing came of it, of course.

Today, fifty years later, I can't think why I didn't just let her leave. I didn't love her enough to beg her to stay. As she herself said, "You don't understand, Axel—how could you understand, you of all people?—but there are parts of my body you have never touched, you don't know the sounds I make and would not recognize them if I were with him and you were in the next room, and you have never ever come close to . . ."

She did not finish the sentence, but I knew exactly what she was talking about. It disgusted me, this . . . what she expected of me, what she had every right to expect of me, what she had found with someone else.

I dreaded the nights. Came up with degrading excuses, degrading both for her and for me, to get out of it. Of course sometimes I had to, and sometimes I forced myself to, but always with her on top, astride me, since that way I did not have to touch her, and I knew full well that *that* way it would all be over much quicker, that her tense little shudders would not be long in coming. And when that happened, the shuddering, it was all over. Even though she would have liked it to last longer, it was over. That was all I waited for, shut my eyes, waited, barely aware of her going through her solitary dance, far away, above me, waited for what I could, with good conscience, call the end.

"You got what you wanted," I told her on one occasion when she tried to lull me into carrying on. "Don't you think I can feel you shuddering?"

She repeated the word, seeming almost surprised. "Did you say shuddering?"

She looked me straight in the eye.

"Shuddering!"

Then she laughed softly and turned her back on me.

"That's only my body betraying me," she whispered. "Don't fool yourself, Axel, it certainly isn't pleasure."

I MEET NO ONE I know on the way to the crematorium, although the young news vendor with the blank eyes is at her post. I've lived in this city all my life, and still it seems foreign to me. I walk past the station building at Majorstuen. There were plans, at one time, for this building to be an imposing landmark, a taller and grander edifice than the one that stands on this spot today; a good-sized skyscraper was more what town planner Harald Hals had had in mind. But then came the war, and all the plans for a fine city bit the dust. Oslo seems to have this in common with my own life: Nothing turns out as planned.

For instance, it had never occurred to me that Gerd might die before me. In good moments, I used to envisage a peaceful old age with her, thinking that in time we could become good friends, she and I, once her appetite had abated. Or that God, if he exists, would grant me an early release, and in her old age she could have a nice life with her women friends and her visits to the theater.

And Stella! I cannot explain this thing with Stella! To fall like that, to stumble over the edge, with her own husband, that conceited ass, as witness? I cannot understand it. So careless. So pointless. What were they doing up there on the roof? Such a damned clumsy thing for a damned clumsy woman to do, fooling around high up in the air. Clumsy people have certain obligations, to themselves and to their bodies and to other people. Clumsy people are always apt to bring accidents in their wake if they're not careful. I should know. I myself am a clumsy man.

Stella Descending

Let's imagine, Bee, that we're climbing up some scaffolding, a steeple, or up onto a roof just like Mamma and Martin. We can see the whole city spread out before us; then we count one, two, three, and we jump. (But first I've got to make love with Snip, Snap, and Snout; I've got to hear them whisper sweet things in my ear about my breasts and my belly and my face while they take me from the front and from behind, because one thing's for sure: I don't intend to be a virgin when I jump.) We'll jump, and our dresses will fill with air so they look like two balloons, two red balloons, and after a while we too will meet the birds and the squirrel and the cod and the old woman. Who knows, we might even see old Granny drifting down through the air with her wispy hair standing on end, and if we fall even faster we're bound to meet Mamma, too, somewhere between heaven and earth; just you wait and see.

(II)

FALL

Frederikke Moll
Witness

There are a man and a woman on the roof. She's wearing a red-and-yellow summer dress—the sort of dress I make myself—and she has strawberry-blond hair. Red sandals on her feet.

There's not a lot I can tell you. I can't even answer the simplest question of all: Does he try to save her or does he push her over the edge? You'd think I could say for sure one way or the other. They embrace, they're standing with their arms wrapped around each other way up there, and just as I'm thinking to myself, Now *there's* a couple in love, she falls. Nine stories, straight down. I shut my eyes, step back, scream—they embrace and then she falls, that's all I know. But as to the question—Did he try to save her or did he push her over the edge?—I couldn't say. It couldn't be both. He couldn't both stop her and push her. To do that he'd have to grab hold of her with his right hand and push with the left, or grab hold of her with his left hand and push with the right. A sort of a contest between hands, maybe, the good hand and the bad. If the investigating officer, an odd, darkly brooding sort of woman, were to ask me to describe him—she hasn't done this, she has only asked me to describe what I saw—but if she were to ask me to describe or identify him, I couldn't. All I remember is her. A yellow-and-red summer dress, yellow-and-red fabric unfurling in the breeze, unfurling into more and more fabric. Over and over again it happens—they embrace and she falls—for this is a moment that is bound to be relived time and time again, and there is nothing I can do to prevent it.

Night after night I am woken by an embrace, a scream that is both hers and mine, by yellow-and-red fabric unfurling. I sit up, half asleep, drenched in sweat and so very, very tired.

Corinne

It was the middle of the night, and Martin Vold had talked and talked. We sat on either side of the big dark-brown dining table. I am a good listener. My sense organs are in excellent working order: my ears, my mouth, my hands, my eyes, and my well-endowed nose. Thanks to my nose, I can tell by the smell of a man whether he has committed a crime. That comes in handy in my line of work. My fellow police officers tell me it's a good thing I'm not married, because any husband of mine would have a hard life.

I would smell it on him every time he was unfaithful to me. I would smell it on him every time he lied. I would smell it on him every time he toyed with the idea of doing away with me.

But then again, I'm at least five hundred years old and weigh about as many kilos, so marriage has never really been in the cards for me.

"'The difference between you and me, Martin, is that you were loved as a child.' Let's dwell on that sentence, Martin."

Martin nodded. I continued.

"You were sitting on the sofa over there." I pointed to the green sofa. "And Stella was sitting cross-legged on the floor. Suddenly she lost her temper, jumped to her feet, and announced that the difference between you and her was that you were loved as a child. Can you picture the scene?"

"But why did she lose her temper?" Martin asked.

"You'd been discussing the children."

Martin was silent. Then he whispered, almost to himself, "Well, no wonder she lost her temper."

"Is that true, then? Were you loved as a child?"

"The world's full of children who are loved. What the hell does that mean, for a child to be loved? Is my daughter, Bee, loved? Let me tell you my story. I grew up in Høylandet. My father's name was Jesper, my mother's name was Nora. But that doesn't answer your question. My family have been farmers for generations. My great-grandfather on my father's side was Swedish, and he and his wife had the northernmost ostrich farm in the world. We still raise ostriches. The person I take after most is my grandfather Elias. He didn't want to be like the rest of the family. He wasn't interested in ostriches. He wanted to be a movie star. He certainly had the looks for it; there wasn't a finer-looking man in the whole of Scandinavia. But he was killed by a train; so much for *that* movie career.

"Back home in Høylandet his intended, Harriet, was pregnant with my father. Elias had treated her shamefully, running off like that with no intention of ever coming back . . . but back he came anyway, in a coffin, sliced in two. Not quite what Harriet had hoped, maybe, but she wasn't the type to wallow in grief and soon got over it. They do say she really let him have it, once he was six feet under and no longer in a position to defend himself. Some people think she put a curse on him. It's mainly because of her . . . it's mainly because of Harriet that Stella said I was loved as a child. My parents are good honest human beings, but that's about as much as I can say for them."

"But your grandmother, Harriet, loved you?"

"I guess it would be truer to say that I loved *her*. Loved her with all my heart."

"You loved your grandmother with all your heart?"

"Yes."

"Because?"

"Because my grandmother . . ."

"Yes?"

"When I was six, I used to spend the night at her house. I often spent the night there. I loved everything about my grandma. She was a great cook, she wore her hair in a long gray braid that swung back and forth over her behind when she was pottering about in the garden, and she had a gentleman friend called Thorleif, a retired accountant with Portuguese blood in him. To be honest, she didn't really have much time for me. She loved me as much as she should, no more, no less. As much as she should. Do you know what I'm saying?"

"I think so."

"One evening Grandma sent me to bed early. I had had my bath and eaten my supper in the kitchen: fresh-baked rolls and hot chocolate with cream. It was always the same at Grandma's, always some tasty treat in the kitchen. When I was tucked in for the night, she sat on the edge of my bed and let me stroke her face. There was nothing I liked better than stroking Grandma's face, and that night she even brought her face down to mine and whispered, 'You're going to be every bit as handsome as your grandpa, maybe more, but let's hope you won't be as stupid. Your grandpa ran off with his head full of dreams: the theater, steam trains, and women. Theater, trains, and women, that's all I ever heard about. But he paid the price.' Grandma kissed my cheek. 'You won't leave me, Martin, will you?' I shook my head. She smiled at me, ruffled my hair. Then she got up and left. I lay there in the dark, longing for her. I wondered whether I dared call her back and ask for one more kiss, but I knew that would make her angry. That much I knew. In the end, I crept out of bed and padded to the kitchen, where I had eaten supper earlier. I knew that Grandma was preparing a joint for roasting. I could easily hide behind the coats that hung on a hook in the hall, right next to the kitchen, and watch her, the braid swinging back and forth, back and forth over her behind. So there I stood, behind the coats, longing for her, worshiping her, wanting her with all my six-year-old heart. All of a sudden I heard footsteps behind me and I shrank back, making myself as small as I could. If I was found there she would ignore me for the whole of the next day, and there was no punishment worse than that. She might even decide to send me home earlier than planned. I heard footsteps. It was Thorleif, and Thorleif also stood there, looking at her. Now there were two of us. She bent down to put the joint in the oven. And that glorious sight—Grandma bent down over the oven, the braid hanging down her back, rump in the air—was too much for Thorleif. He unbuttoned his fly and made a run at her, flung up her skirt, and fell on her. Bad idea! The joint landed on the floor, Grandma hit her head on the edge of the oven and burned her left cheek, and Thorleif fell and broke his arm.

"They were both yelling and cursing, and Grandma hit Thorleif in the face with a saucepan. As for me, I tiptoed back to bed and snuggled up under the eiderdown. I was so grateful, I really was. I had seen true love. Harriet, the loveliest lass in all Høylandet, wasn't just my grandma, she was a goddess."

Video Recording: Stella & Martin
The House by the Lady Falls
8/27/00, 3:50 A.M.

MARTIN: Stella's not saying anything. She thinks we should
               do this some other way, don't you, Stella? You
               think we should do this some other way. She's
               shaking her head. Now she's sticking her tongue
               out. Want to see? She's sitting on the floor with
               her legs curled under her, playing with the silver
               locket that belonged to her mother. Would you like
               to see my wife's tongue? I'm going to immortalize
               that tongue, I'm going to immortalize that tongue
               right now, that little pink tongue that reminds me
               of . . . shall I tell you what your tongue reminds me
               of, Stella?

STELLA: Do I have any choice?

MARTIN: Oh, we always have a choice.

STELLA: Axel doesn't think we can choose. He thinks—

MARTIN: Axel's a senile old fool.

STELLA: He is *not* senile! Look, are you going to tell me
               what my tongue reminds you of, or are you going

to do this properly, because if you are then I think
we should start with the silverware or something
like that.

MARTIN: Your tongue, Stella. Stick it out. That's it. Way out.
Like a kid at the doctor saying *aaahhh*. Your tongue
reminds me of a fine fillet of fish, redfish or catfish,
marinated in olive oil, garlic, and white wine,
grilled and served with no accompaniment other
than a bottle of dry white wine, suitably chilled.

STELLA: You're making me hungry.

MARTIN: For your own tongue? Isn't there a saying about
that: Bite your tongue?

STELLA: One of my patients almost bit off her tongue
because it hurt so much.

MARTIN: What hurt so much?

STELLA: Dying. She was screaming and begging and
threatening to bite big chunks off of herself if we
didn't help her.

MARTIN: Did you help her?

STELLA: Yes.

MARTIN: But it didn't help?

STELLA: No.

MARTIN: Still hungry?

STELLA: No.

MARTIN: Okay, then I can tell you where I ate a fillet of fish
like that, the sort your tongue reminds me of. It
was in Italy. Before—long before—I met you. It
was in the evening. I was at this ramshackle little
restaurant somewhere on the Amalfi coast, sitting

outside, under the lemon trees. The owner said the wine was on him, and he came to the table personally, to show us the fish he was thinking of having the chef prepare.

STELLA: Us?

MARTIN: Us?

STELLA: You said: He came over to the table personally to show *us*. Who's us?

MARTIN: This was before your time, before you and me.

STELLA: You and me. You and her. Who exactly were you eating fish with under the lemon trees?

MARTIN: The lovely Penelope.

STELLA: Penelope?

MARTIN: Penelope.

STELLA: And who is Penelope?

MARTIN: Penelope happened long before you.

STELLA: So what you're saying is that every time I make a face at you . . .

MARTIN: And every time you kiss me . . .

STELLA: And every time I pop a little dumpling in your mouth . . .

MARTIN: And every time I lick you until you're wet . . .

STELLA: And every time I sleep with my mouth open . . .

MARTIN: And every time you stick the tip of your tongue between the cheeks of my ass . . .

STELLA: You think of a whore named Penelope.

MARTIN: No, I think of the fillet of fish I once had in a restaurant in Italy, which I just happened to eat with Penelope sitting next to me.

STELLA: But indirectly, my tongue reminds you of another woman.

MARTIN: Indirectly, your tongue reminds me that you talk too much. . . . My wife talks too much. You'll have to excuse her. Allow me to tell you a little bit about the sofa on which she is sitting. The avocado-green sofa: This is where it all began. It might be stained and worn now, but it cost a fortune once upon a time, and we wouldn't know what to do with ourselves if we ever lost it. The thing is, you see, that this sofa, this avocado-green sofa in our living room, here in Martin and Stella's living room, is a magic sofa. Magic, my dear Mr. Insurance Broker, Mr.—what was his name again?

STELLA: His name was . . . now I remember! His name was Owesen, Gunnar R. Owesen. That was his name.

MARTIN: Right. Mr. Gunnar R. Owesen, insurance broker. He's our man if our house goes up in flames or if we're burglarized or hit by some other appalling catastrophe. Take a look at this video and you'll see that we've got all of our stuff on film now—just like you said—everything of value, right? We've described it all and put a price on it all. And I'm here to tell you: This sofa is magic. Have you ever sat on a magic sofa? I think not. I don't mean to underestimate you or your experience, but I don't think you've ever sat on a magic sofa, I don't think magic sofas exist in your insurance man's . . . in your well-insured world. Stella and I were just talking about you. We talked about you the day you

came to look at our house. We were trying to
imagine what sort of life you must lead, what you
dream about at night. We think you're on the
lookout for something else: another wife, for
example, another job. You see, the thing is, Gunnar
R. Owesen, the very first time you sit down on that
sofa you are granted one wish—you can wish for
almost anything in the world—and *presto!* your
wish will be granted. But this offer is only valid the
very first time you sit on it. Never again. You can
sit down on that sofa a hundred times, two hundred
times, three hundred times, and you can wish all
you want, but it won't do any good. It's only the
first time that counts. When Stella and I have
guests—which, to be honest, is not very often; the
house is full enough as it is, what with plumbers
and kids—but when we have guests or other
callers, like yourself for example, Mr. Gunnar R.
Owesen, we might well invite you to sit on the sofa,
we might well bring the conversation round to the
question of what one wants out of life, and then we
would ask you what you would like most of all.
And after you've given it some thought, just as you
are about to answer, Stella chimes in—

STELLA: Ssh. Don't say it out loud. If you want your wish to
come true, it has to be kept secret.

MARTIN: We don't tell you that you're sitting on a magic
sofa. That's *our* secret. It's just a game, right? You
laugh and take another sip of coffee or wine,
depending on whether it's daytime or evening, and
Stella and I try to read your expression, to find out
what you wished for. Was it a nice wish or a nasty
one? Because the sofa grants all wishes, not just
the nice ones.

Stella Descending

STELLA: The first time I sat on the sofa . . .

MARTIN: The first time you sat on the sofa, I thought . . .

STELLA: The first time I sat on the sofa, I thought: I want this sofa!

MARTIN: The first time you sat on the sofa, I thought: I want you. You see, Mr. Insurance Broker Gunnar R. Owesen, it was this sofa, this avocado-green sofa, that brought us together. Stella walked into the Galileo furniture store, sat down on this sofa, turned to me, and said, *I want this one.* Six weeks later I delivered it to her home.

STELLA: He put it down in the middle of the living room. And then he refused to leave.

MARTIN: You didn't want me to leave, Stella.

STELLA: Everybody just stays.

MARTIN: Poor Stella.

STELLA: Everybody just stays: Martin; Herr Poppel, the plumber.

MARTIN: Don't tell me you're going to start complaining about Herr Poppel now, too?

STELLA: I don't know whether his face is nice or nasty.

MARTIN: Whenever I see Herr Poppel's face it makes me think of my grandma Harriet.

STELLA: A nasty face, then.

MARTIN: No, Stella, a nice face.

STELLA: She hits children, you know.

MARTIN: Stella, not that story again.

Corinne

I have three witnesses: Alma Blom, Frederikke Moll, and Ella Dalby. Three women in black coming into my office, each one uglier than the one before, and each of them with some bit of knitting in her hands. There were other people around, obviously; it was a warm sunny evening, the apartment house faces Frogner Park, and there were people everywhere—waiting for the streetcar or entering the park, people with picnic baskets, dogs, bottles of wine, footballs—but Oslo is not a city where people are in the habit of craning their necks and looking up. Oslo is a city where people look either straight ahead or at the ground, which is why no one ever notices the things that are forever happening high up above.

So a crowd of people came running after the fall, when Stella was lying on the ground, covered by the fleecy blue traveling rug that Alma Blom, one of the witnesses, had thrown over her in horror. A crowd came running after it happened, but only three saw her before the fall, up there on the roof with Martin.

Stella and Martin on the roof, nine stories above the ground, back and forth along the edge, first him, then her, tiny steps, arms out to the sides like circus performers, tightrope walkers, equilibrists. Alma Blom, or maybe it was Frederikke Moll, calls to them to get down from there, but they do not hear. Instead they teeter toward each other, fling their arms around each other, and stay like that for a while, in a sort of embrace.

Although Alma Blom maintains that this embrace was more like a tussle.

Martin and I were sitting at the table. I said, "Your wife was pregnant, Martin. Three or four weeks gone."

Martin spread his arms wide. "That can't be true," he said. "She was on the pill."

"It's true." I sighed. "My friend Karina down at pathology found a yellowish mass less than a centimeter long in her womb, an embryo." I show Martin the nail of my index finger. "Smaller than this nail, just a little bit of a thing. A bulge in the mucous membrane, my friend Karina said, a spongy little blob, an excrescence. Did you know?"

"No."

"You didn't know she was pregnant?"

"No, I said."

"Did you want to have more children?"

"No."

"Did Stella want to have more children?"

"No, I told you, she was on the pill."

Amanda

When Mamma was sick we thought she was going to die. Mamma thought it was pathetic, all those books she hadn't read, so I sat in her hospital room and read her this book about a captain who sails the ocean hunting a sea monster. We didn't get very far before Mamma couldn't take any more, which was fine by me. After a while, all she wanted me to read was the real estate pages in *Aftenposten*.

"You know," she said, "I think if we were to move from the house we're living in now to another house, we'd be able to start all over again," and then she hugged me.

I asked her why we would want to start all over again when we had already come so far. I for one didn't want to start all over again, round all those worlds again, I said.

She said it was just a figure of speech, not meant to be taken literally.

I said I knew that.

One day I read about an apartment on Frognerveien. I don't remember whether it was for sale or for rent. We read both the FOR SALE and the FOR RENT ads, in the morning and evening editions.

"Oh," said Mamma. "That's where we lived before we moved

into our house. The same building. I wonder whether it's our old apartment."

I remember when we lived there.

Once, a long time ago, long before Mamma was born even, a man climbed up onto the roof of that building and jumped off. Mamma told me this when she was explaining why I shouldn't lean out the windows. It's no wonder; we *were* living on the ninth floor. I can see why she was worried. I was only four or five then, a runny-nosed little kid.

"No one, Amanda, no one. No one knows why he jumped," Mamma said.

Corinne

"There's another sentence I'd like us to dwell on a little," I told Martin.

He looked away. He got up from the dining table and asked if I would like some coffee. I prefer tea.

"A cup of tea, please," I said. "I never say no to a cup of tea." My fellow officers prefer whisky. Time was, when we were often away on police business, we used to sit up late into the night in hotel rooms, tossing ideas back and forth. 'Yep, a lot of cases have been solved over a glass of Dawson's,' the guys in the team are fond of saying, sounding vaguely wistful. I'd say instead that a lot of cases would have remained unsolved had it not been for a strong cup of Lipton's. But then again, that's just me.

Martin came back with tea.

"This sentence on which you wanted to dwell," he asked. "Which one would that be?"

"Something one of the witnesses said," I replied. "She said that your embrace up there on the roof might just as easily have been a tussle."

Martin glanced away. "No, there was no tussle. It was an embrace. She balanced against me, giddy with the sun, the view, and a sudden . . . joy. And it rubbed off on me. We'd been having a rough time of it."

"Rough in what way?"

"Stella's illness, her mother's death . . . lots of things."

"But things between you two were fine?"

"She drove me crazy," he blurted out. "Stella was so afraid. Afraid of this, afraid of that, and most of all afraid I would leave her. Fearful and tight-lipped. She was a child. Like Bee."

"Bee is your daughter?"

"You have to take your children on trust."

"Meaning?"

"Meaning she's probably mine."

"And now there was another child on the way."

"No!"

"Okay, let me repeat the question: Could that embrace up there on the roof have been a tussle?"

"Everything was just fine between Stella and me. I didn't push her, if that's what you're asking. We were standing there on the edge, close, really close together. I remember running my fingers down her long slim back, the fine fabric of her dress, her backbone under my fingertips. When I was a little boy, Thorleif, my grandma's gentleman friend, told me that my grandmother's back reminded him of a Stradivarius. Before he became an accountant in Høylandet, Thorleif had actually been a musician, a violinist, with only one great dream in life: to get the chance, just once, to play a Stradivarius. He never got to do it; I don't think he was a particularly good musician. As I was stroking Stella's back, this childhood memory swept through me like a puff of blue smoke," Martin said.

He considered me for a moment.

"I didn't push her," he repeated.

I said, "Tell me about the video."

"The video," he said.

"Yes," I said. "The video."

"Our neighbor had a break-in during the winter, and he wasn't insured. We felt that we ought to be insured, or at least Stella, who was always so afraid of everything, was adamant that we ought to be insured. The insurance broker came over, went from room to room making notes, and then told us he usually advised anyone taking out an insurance policy to get all the items of value in the house down on video, with a running commentary, in case it all went up in flames or got stolen. He said that when disaster strikes, people tend to forget what they had and what it was worth." Martin laughed. "But nothing much came of that insurance video," he said.

"Oh. Well . . . it makes interesting viewing," I remarked.

We sat in silence for a while. The silence was getting on his nerves. The silence gave me the upper hand. He drummed on the table with his fingers.

"What are you thinking?" he asked eventually.

"I was thinking about the sofa," I said. "That's it there, isn't it?" A sliding door divided the room in two. We were sitting in the dining area, and the green sofa was in the living area.

"It's not often that people in my line of work have anything to do with magic sofas. I once had a case involving a flying carpet, but a magic sofa . . . never! I don't suppose you would let me sit on it, so I could make a wish?"

"What would you wish for?" Martin asked.

"Ah, that I can't tell you."

Martin produced a pack of cigarettes and offered me one, but I turned it down. He lit up and sat there gazing at the smoke rings he was blowing.

"I don't think anyone as fat as you has ever sat on it," he said.

"D'you want to see it break in two?"

"Just like my grandfather," he says.

"The man who lay down on the railroad tracks?"

"Yeah, him."

Again we fell silent. I had plenty of time. My fellow officers never take their time. I tell them: You have to take your time. But taking things slow scares them, as does silence. I pulled a nail file from my purse and proceeded to file my nails. I have exceptionally beautiful hands. If you saw me, your first thought would be that there isn't anything beautiful about me, not one single thing. But that would be because you hadn't noticed my hands.

For a long time not a word was spoken. Martin stared at the ceiling. I filed my nails. The dining table stretched out between us. To lighten things up a little I suggested that we tell each other stories. A police detective and a furniture salesman must have plenty to say, and there's no reason why circumstances, in this case an unexplained death, should prevent two people from getting better acquainted. The other detectives on the squad feel I waste too much time on stories that are not really relevant. But I tell them it is there, in the small talk, in the idle chitchat, in the little asides, that the solution lies.

"Yeah, right, Corrie," they say. "You and Miss Marple!"

And I say, "Trust me. There is an order to this. Faint, I grant you, but no less human for all that."

So I told Martin about a case I had a long time ago.

"How long ago?" he asked.

"Almost a hundred years," I said.

He nodded.

"Once upon a time there was a man not unlike you in manner and looks. This man was such a good liar that it was impossible to catch him out," I said. "I had no proof, just a suspicion, a twinge in my stomach. And besides, I could smell it. I can, you know," I told him. "I can smell whether a man is guilty or innocent."

"You don't say," Martin replied, making no move to pull farther away from me.

"On that occasion I didn't even have a body," I continued. "I did, however, have three hundred and fifty-eight witnesses, quite literally an audience. On the night when a conjurer of some repute magicked his wife away for good.

"This conjurer, who went by the name of El Jabali, was considered to be one of the best in Scandinavia. As a boy he had dreamed of becoming the new Houdini. Spurred on by the idea of being able to wriggle out of even the trickiest situations—chains, blocks of ice, a sea of flame, you name it—he eventually managed to worm his way into the good graces of the top magicians in Norway, from whom he tried to pick up a few pointers. He was a quick study and was soon performing at functions and parties all over the country, doing tricks with cards, dice, silk scarves, a top hat, two doves, and a rabbit. But he was no Houdini. He practiced and practiced, but he could never get out of his self-imposed restraints quickly enough, never succeeded in presenting himself to the audience as a free man, a living declaration: I exist! I am! When, at the age of twenty-three, he finally recognized that his dream of becoming the new Houdini was never going to come true, he was miserable. For four years he remained miserable. He lay under the eiderdown in his lodgings in Majorstua, feeling miserable and wishing only that he could disappear. His landlady threatened to throw him out. His parents threatened to cut him off without a penny. His friends threatened to deny him solace and financial support. Then two things happened. Toward the end of the fourth year he started to think; he hitched his demons to his cart and made *them* work for *him* instead of the other way round. He summoned all the beasts of his depression and asked them, How can I become the world's greatest conjurer? And the beasts replied as they always had: You do not exist! You are not!

"For four years El Jabali had lain under his eiderdown wishing he could disappear. And to some extent he had succeeded. No one spoke to him anymore. No one cared about him. No one gave him a second thought. And then it came to him in a flash: His destiny was not to become the new Houdini; it was not to present himself to the whole world, proclaiming I exist! I am! Quite the opposite. His destiny as a conjurer, as a magician, as El Jabali, was to make things disappear: cards, dice, silk scarves, top hats, doves, rabbits, maybe even a beautiful woman, and finally, of course, himself.

"A little flourish, he thought, and everything is plunged into darkness. Everything disappears.

"Toward the end of his four years under the eiderdown, two things happened to El Jabali. One was that he started thinking. The other was that once he took up with his friends again, he met a half-Russian, half-Congolese circus artiste named Darling and fell in love with her. Darling returned his love, and not long after their first tempestuous encounter, they were married. Darling's father was a ringmaster, and El Jabali promptly became a natural part of his father-in-law's small but well-established Circus Bravado. Every night he performed a number of conventional conjuring tricks—entertaining enough, but nothing really sensational. Not yet.

"Then the Circus Bravado set out on its tour of Norway. For the young newlyweds life was, on the whole, pretty good. Everyone knew that El Jabali was cooking something up. Before every show he would lie on his bed in the trailer he shared with Darling, listening to Schubert's *Die Winterreise* and contemplating his grand disappearing act. Eventually he got around to telling his wife about his plans: how he could make absolutely anything vanish without trace right before the very eyes of the audience, just like that—no cabinet, no trapdoor, no fluttering draperies, nothing—simply the most stupendous optical illusion, a gradual fade-out, right there in the middle of the ring, in front of hundreds of astonished witnesses. Darling took to the idea immediately and offered to be his assistant.

"Darling was a trapeze artist. She had grown up in the circus. It was not in her nature to be anyone's assistant. This half-Russian, half-Congolese girl was a diva by the age of nine, when she was the top of a human pyramid consisting of her grandfather and grandmother, father and mother, five brothers, two sisters, three boy cousins, and one girl cousin. Darling had faith in her husband's talents as a magician. He had the hands for it, good hands. There was no doubt in Darling's mind that he had a magician's hands. But she was also prepared to be his assistant for another reason: She dreaded his black moods, which some-times threatened to send them both plummeting into the abyss, so she was more than willing to vanish from the ring a little at a time, once a night, to the entrancing sound of the audience's applause—if that was what it took to make him happy.

"His disappearing act was a sensation from the very first show, and the press was soon hailing El Jabali as the greatest magician in Scandinavia. The Circus Bravado's tour of Norway proved to be its most successful ever, and El Jabali's father-in-law, the ringmaster, finally seemed pleased with his son-in-law, slapped him on the back, and kissed him on the lips. Not another word was said about the fact that in the past the ringmaster had been known to refer to his son-in-law in somewhat derogatory terms—calling him a conceited ass, for example. But then El Jabali really was presenting the Bravado's audiences with a most amazing conjuring trick."

"Can you describe it?" Martin asked. The room was dark; his face, across the dining table, indistinct.

"Close your eyes and picture it," I said.

Martin didn't close his eyes, but he listened quietly never-theless.

"The show is almost over. The lights are low, only a single pool of white light in the center of the ring. The pianist plays the first stanzas of what a few people will recognize as the last song in Schubert's cycle *Die Winterreise*. El Jabali wanders into the ring, dressed like a tramp, a clownish musician in a squashed top hat, a moth-eaten dinner suit, a tattered bow tie, and a pair of enormous black shoes. He shuffles in, heading for the pool of light, stopping now and then to cock his head and point to the circus orchestra, as if to tell the audience that he too can hear the piano music.

"Then he is standing perfectly still in the pool of light. He casts a wary glance at the pianist before proceeding to turn his right arm in a circle. The pianist plays and the tramp's arm turns. And so it goes. The pianist plays; the tramp's arm turns.

Eventually two clowns dressed in red run into the ring, carrying a barrel organ. They set it down gently in front of the tramp and indicate with their huge whitened hands that he can play it if he wants; the barrel organ is a gift from them to him. Then they run out.

"So the tramp plays the barrel organ, one little tune after another, but he doesn't seem too happy. He looks around. He's all alone. Even the clowns have gone. No one wants to listen to the organ grinder. But maybe if he plays something else—yes, that's it, maybe if he plays something else—and so he does, something a bit livelier, as if he were summoning someone, calling out to someone, and to the audience's amazement a woman begins to materialize in the pool of light. First one arm, then another arm, then a finger, then an eye, a knee, a foot, a toe, then one breast, followed by another. From out of nowhere there she is, a dazzlingly beautiful young woman, half Russian, half Congolese, every bit as solid, every bit as alive as the organ grinder himself. Who would have believed it? A woman conjured up out of nothing.

"And then they dance. The organ grinder dances with the woman.

"I can dance, he says. Although, of course, you don't hear him say that because this is a circus act and words are rarely spoken at the circus. But that is what you imagine he is saying: that he can dance. And pride gets the better of him, the tramp is all puffed up with pride. He says he doesn't need to stand here playing his barrel organ because he can dance. He can even dance alone. I can dance just as well without you, he says. I can dance alone in this pool of light.

"The organ grinder raises both hands in the air and gives a little flourish, that's all he does, a flourish, and the beautiful young woman starts to disappear. She dissolves, dematerializes, melts away, right then and there before hundreds of eyes, and it hurts. You can tell from the look on her face. It hurts to disappear like that, against your will, in the middle of the dance; it hurts to be touched out, erased, vaporized, turned to nothing in the presence of all these witnesses.

"She doubles up in pain. And then, like a bubble bursting—before you can so much as blink—she is gone.

"That's pretty much how it went," I concluded.

"And the audience was just as amazed every evening?" Martin asked.

"The audience was just as amazed every evening," I said. "In Kristiansand, Bergen, Stavanger, Trondheim, and Bodø. Well, after all, how did he do it? Conjure up a woman and then magic her away again? It has to be something to do with the barrel organ, somebody says. It has to be something to do with that. But the woman wasn't anywhere near the barrel organ, say others. And yet they saw her with their own eyes, crumbling in the pool of light, turning to dust. All he does is give a little flourish. It has nothing to do with the barrel organ. So the conversation went every evening after the show—and in every town in Norway people flocked to the Circus Bravado to see El Jabali and his incredible disappearing act.

"The tour ended up in Oslo. Nine shows, all sold out. According to witnesses, El Jabali and his wife, Darling, were thrilled and delighted to be such a huge success, not least El Jabali, who was greeted by shouts of *Bravo! Bravo!* every evening when he and Darling ran into the ring to take their bow.

"Then, one evening—the second-to-last show of the summer—El Jabali took his bow without his wife. The audience didn't give it much thought. After all, he was the magician. His wife was only the lady who disappeared, the lady he magicked away. The audience didn't know she was a star in her own right, a trapeze artist, a diva by the age of nine, when she was the top of a pyramid consisting of her grandfather and grandmother, father and mother, five brothers, two sisters, three boy cousins, and one girl cousin. But Darling's father, the ringmaster, knew, and he *did* notice that El Jabali took his bow alone, and he feared his daughter might have gone off in a huff. So after the show, he took a walk around to look for her. He asked the musicians, Have you seen my daughter? And the musicians shook their heads and said no, the last time they saw her was in the ring with El Jabali. So the ringmaster walked on until he came to Star and Moon, the tightrope walkers. He asked the tightrope walkers, Have you seen my daughter? and Star and Moon shook their heads and said no, the last time they saw her was in the ring with El Jabali. So the ringmaster walked on until he came to the lion tamer (who, in fact, only tamed dogs, horses, and a singing ostrich, because they no longer had any lions at the Circus Bravado). And he asked the lion tamer, Have you seen my daughter? The lion tamer shook his head and said no, not since she was in the ring with El Jabali. And then the ringmaster (who just then remembered that he really never did like that son-in-law of his) asked, Where is El Jabali? In a voice like thunder he roared: *Where is El Jabali?* Yes, where is El Jabali? they all asked themselves. Because El Jabali was nowhere to be found. Darling, his wife, the ringmaster's daughter, was nowhere to be found either. Darling had vanished. El Jabali had vanished.

"Soon, however, El Jabali was found. He was sitting on a tree stump outside his caravan, drinking apple juice and eating a sandwich. The ringmaster came dashing up to him, the musicians, the tightrope walkers, the lion tamer, the bookkeeper, the contortionist, the clown, the dogs, and the ostrich hard on his heels, grabbed him by the shoulders, shook him, and demanded to know where his daughter was, demanded to know why his daughter did not take her bow. El Jabali said he didn't know. 'I haven't seen her since I magicked her away.' And weird as it is, this was his story and he stuck to it. The police were called in. On the face of it, there was good reason to suspect that a crime had been committed. I arrived at the scene. I spoke to those present. I spoke to El Jabali. I spoke to everyone who was at the circus the night Darling was magicked away, but none of them could tell me any more than what they believed they had seen with their own eyes: that Darling was magicked away, that she disappeared, melted, and turned to nothing in front of hundreds of witnesses."

"And El Jabali?" Martin asked.

"He disappeared too."

"You never saw him again?"

"Oh, there are times when I think I see him. Unsolved cases tend to haunt me," I said. "He must be an old man by now, if he's still alive."

"Now I'll tell you a story," Martin announced.

"That was the deal," I said.

"I'll tell you about the avocado-green sofa," he said.

"You're not going to tell me it's magic, are you?" I asked. "Because I know that already."

"No, not that," he said. And this is the story Martin told me.

Long ago, before Martin met Stella, he had a girlfriend whose name was Penelope Lund. And one day Penelope told Martin that he was a spineless, shiftless, spoiled, self-centered layabout who didn't deserve the love of a good woman. Martin couldn't argue with that. On the contrary, he had to admit that Penelope was right on all counts. This did not mean he stopped going out with women, by no means. He simply stopped going out with Penelope Lund, for a while at any rate. Instead, he embarked on a long and intoxicating succession of affairs with many different women.

His job as a furniture salesman made it possible for him to expand his romantic repertoire ad infinitum. It is no secret that most furniture is bought by women. No secret, either, that a woman's heart starts to flutter the minute she becomes aware that she's near a store full of beautiful things for her house. So there came a day when the young furniture salesman decided to take advantage of those fluttering hearts and bed every woman (and when I say every woman, Martin stressed, I mean *every woman*) who bought the avocado-green sofa, the one on display near the shop's busy café, the one flanked by a lamp with a white shade like a Victorian lady's bonnet. The very sofa that would in due course bring him to Stella, into Stella's life, into Stella's bed, without a clue that ten years later he would have to explain why Stella should suddenly fall to her death from a roof on an August evening.

The whole point, he explained, was that his choice of women would not, in fact, be his choice. He was in no position to choose for himself, and he didn't want to anyway. Martin decided to have no will of his own. Martin did not intend to make up his own mind about anything, to make any decisions based on his own needs, desires, wishes, urges. Martin intended to take life as it came, a life suspended between heaven and earth, here and there, night and day. But in order to do this, without ending up dead—which would actually be more natural—Martin devised a system, a scheme, a rigid code of conduct. He made up a set of rules for eating and drinking, a set of rules for going to the bathroom, a set of rules for earning and spending money, and a set of rules for meeting women. With these he felt he had covered the necessities. The urges to fill himself, void himself, support himself, and reproduce himself might have led another man to make choices the consequences of which said man would have to live with, knowing full well that these had been his choices, knowing full well that he was responsible for his own downfall. Martin had always been convinced that his downfall was just around the corner, but he preferred not to take responsibility for it. So when it came to women, he might just as well let the sofa choose: Sooner or later, every woman who bought the avocado-green sofa would receive a visit from Martin Vold, sooner or later every one of them would undress for Martin Vold, and sooner or later every one of them would be well and truly and most memorably fucked by Martin Vold. Whether they were ugly or pretty, fat or thin, young or old, bitchy or sweet, it made no difference. He would sleep with all of them.

At this point in the story I couldn't help but interrupt. "But surely there can't be that many women who buy avocado-green sofas?"

"You've no idea," he replied. "It was like a mania with that sofa. Everybody wanted one."

I hesitated slightly before asking my next question. I asked him to forgive me for sounding naive, but didn't it ever happen that some women had their husbands or boyfriends with them when they came to look at furniture, and wouldn't that make it difficult—I glanced at my notes—wouldn't that make it difficult "well and truly and most memorably" to fuck them? "I mean," I said, groping for the words, "what did you do with the man?"

He sighed. "I arranged to deliver the sofa when he wasn't home."

"Did any woman ever say no?"

"No."

"Never?"

"No."

"Have you read Henry Miller?"

"No."

I paused and looked at the ceiling.

"Why?" he asked, uncertainly.

"He wrote somewhere that the male Australian kangaroo has a double penis, one for weekdays and one for holidays. I was wondering if the same applied to you."

He made no answer. He was wondering whether I was making fun of him. Possibly out of curiosity, possibly because we had the whole night ahead of us, I finally asked him to tell me about the women.

"I'd prowl around the store," he said, "spying on them, holding my breath when they went anywhere near the sofa. I took them in—hair, face, breasts, thighs—hoping that this one would sit down on it or that another would walk away. It's a beautiful sofa. It caught the eye of a lot of women. They ran their hands over the soft green fabric, imagining how a sofa like this would look in their own living rooms. Occasionally I might try to influence a customer. Although it was against my rules, if I saw a beautiful girl who, having walked around the sofa, round and round, again and again, finally sat down on it with a rapturous little 'Oohhh, yes!' it wasn't out of the question for me to sidle up to her, shake her hand, and say, 'I think this sofa would look just right in your living room!'

"And the girl would laugh and say, 'But you've no idea how my living room looks, have you?'

"And then I would say that that was exactly what I intended to find out in six to eight weeks, that being Galileo's estimated delivery time."

"Galileo?" I interjected, checking my notes.

"That's the name of the furniture store," Martin explained.

"Of course!"

"We supply tables, chairs, carpets, beds, blinds, lamps, chaise longues, shelving units, closets, benches, writing desks, and pouffes, *and* we serve the best espresso and arugula salad in town."

"Go on, please."

Martin took a deep breath.

"But if a really ugly woman dumped herself on the sofa and indicated that she was interested in it, I would come over, shake my head, and point to another model on display, also Italian. I'd do my best to persuade this woman that the other sofa was a much more attractive piece of furniture, and much cheaper and she ought to go for it instead. I didn't always manage to persuade her. Sometimes the ugly woman had her heart set on the avocado-green sofa, no matter what I said, and then, according to my rules, I had no choice but to serve her, both one way and the other."

"Okay, but come on, it's not as if anyone were forcing you to go through with this," I pointed out. "Least of all these supposedly ugly women—"

"I had a system," he said, butting in, "and I wouldn't give in until—" (He eyed me up and down.) "It's like building a house of cards. To begin with it's just a bit of fun and it doesn't matter if the cards come tumbling down. You merely start again from scratch. But then, after a while, you're getting somewhere. Soon you've got one floor on top of another, and then one more on top of that, and your house is still standing! And then all at once it becomes so fucking vital that it shouldn't fall down—do you know what I mean?—that you should manage to use up all fifty-two cards. That's what it was like. It started as a bet, with a guy at work, maybe, or a friend, that I could seduce the first woman to buy that avocado-green sofa, no matter who she was. And it was the easiest thing in the world. Then the next one, right? Just as easy. And the next, and the next, and the next. And the house was still standing! And with every woman the tension grew that much greater. What if one of them said no? But none of them said no. Not *one* of them said no. And it never occurred to me that *I* might back down, that I might deliberately bring down the house of cards myself, just because I didn't feel attracted to this woman or that."

Once, he told me, a woman came into the shop, walked straight over to the green sofa, and sat down on it. She was small and thin and pale, with a mousy perm curling around a face that did not arouse the slightest feeling in him: dry skin, thin lips, button nose, and small, listless green eyes. "She wasn't at all attractive, but she wasn't downright ugly either. I preferred the really ugly ones," he says, "the spectacularly weird-looking or grossly overweight." (He gave me a look, eyeing my body. I gave him to understand, also by a look, that he couldn't faze me.) This woman, neither attractive nor ugly, bought the avocado-green sofa and received Martin at her apartment eight weeks later. What was to happen next had already been agreed between them, so after she had helped him put the sofa in its place in the living room, next door to the kitchen, she proceeded to undress. She did not look at him. Not even when she lay back on the green cushions did she look at him. He undid his fly and considered the possibility of stroking her cheek, a caress, a word at least, but he dropped the idea, climbed on top of her, and stuck his dick inside her. She might as well have been dead from the waist down, he said; I felt nothing, nothing. But then the woman fixed her gaze on him, forcing him to look into her eyes, eyes filled with tears of joy, the eyes of a happy woman, and he stared at her, entranced by that look, until it dawned on him that he could close his eyes, and so he closed his eyes.

The woman screamed with desire, moving her body in a way that had nothing to do with Martin's body. He tried to find her rhythm, but to no avail, because she didn't care about him. In a flash it came to him: She gazed at him with joyous eyes, screamed with desire, and tossed from side to side, but she didn't care about him. When she came she dug her nails into his back and her body became so taut that she all but pushed him out of her. Then she kissed him for the first time, clinging to him in such a way that he was forced, reluctantly, to bury his nose in that thin hair.

Once they were dressed, she put her arms around him again, flirtatiously now, playfully, like the young heroine of some Victorian novelette who has at long last surrendered to her wooer; she stroked his thigh coquettishly and said something to the effect that it was nice when two people could be together like this. He pulled away when her hand touched him.

"I felt like throwing up. Usually women turn me on; it turns me on to see exactly what will drive this one or that one wild. Sometimes I try to guess in advance, but more often than not I'm wrong. What fascinates me is the way that every woman is different."

"But on this occasion you felt like throwing up. Why was that?"

"I don't know. It was awful. To be honest, I felt like getting up, right in the middle of the act, and telling her I just couldn't be bothered."

"Why didn't you?"

"Out of politeness, I think."

"So after that did you give up seducing women who bought the green sofa?"

"No."

"You still did it?"

"I still did it. The comparison with the house of cards wasn't carelessly made. That was how I saw it. It was like I was building a house of cards. When fifty-two women had bought the avocado-green sofa, when I'd finished building my house and that house stood firm, then I would stop."

"And start again, with new rules?"

"Yes. New rules."

"Seduce women who bought—what—recliners, maybe?"

"Maybe."

"And Stella. You delivered the sofa and you stayed with her for ten years, until she fell off the roof."

"Yes."

"You delivered the sofa, and you stayed."

"I stayed."

Amanda

Bee's asleep now. She'll sleep until Martin knocks on the door and says it's time to go. While the minister is talking in the chapel today I'm going to say *damn, cunt, cock, kill, shit, bloody, cunt, fuck, screw*. Then I won't have to hear what he says. And afterward Pappa will be there, so Martin says. Maybe he'll be waiting outside the chapel for me. I don't know how I feel about Pappa. I've only met him a few times. The first time was when I was three days old. I was asleep, curled up like a cat in the crook of his arm. That's what Mamma told me. Then he went to Australia. I don't know if I miss him; I don't really know him. But Australia's probably nice. Once, before Mamma met Martin, when I was four or maybe five, Pappa came to see us. That was when Mamma and I were living in the apartment on Frognerplass. He kept hugging me. I thought it was horrible. I don't like people hugging me. But he'd brought a whole bag of candy, not one of those little paper bags, but a shopping bag, the kind you get at the supermarket, and the whole bag was full of candy. The shopping bag and the candy both came from Australia.

I used to pretend that the plumber was my father. But now I'd rather have him as my boyfriend. One time, not that long ago, I went up to his room in the attic and asked him if he would make love to me. He was in his bed, asleep. It was pretty late. Mamma and Martin were sleeping. The plumber opened his eyes and looked at me. He switched on his bedside lamp. The light shone straight onto my breasts. I was shivering. I wanted to climb into his bed, under the eiderdown, and curl up close to him. The warmth there. "I think you should go back to bed," he said, very softly. "But I want to get into *your* bed," I said. "No," he said, "that's not a good idea."

Sometimes we play Nintendo, the plumber and I. He killed the beast in the forest and rounded the most difficult world of all. That's what we call it when we complete a level. We round one world and move on to the next. I would never have managed to round that world on my own. And sometimes he does let me into his bed. Then we make love all night and his stuff's pouring out of me all the next day. There was this one time in class when Marianne started giggling. I was going around the desks, handing out an English test. Marianne was giggling, then the girl sitting next to Marianne, whose name is Vigdis, she started giggling, and soon the whole class was giggling. I was wearing light-colored pants. I knew my panties were wet and sticky— they'd been like that all day—but I didn't think it would show. Everyone said I'd wet myself or gotten my period. That wasn't exactly it, as I told Marianne afterward at break.

By the way, I'm not in love with him. The plumber, I mean. I have other lovers, too.

Bee's asleep. Bee is lying here next to me. She looks like a doll with her long dark hair and her red dress. She has a red raincoat, too, with a hood, and red rubber boots. Today the sun is shining, though. It could at least be raining, seeing as we're going to bury Mamma. Maybe Bee's dreaming about Mamma. Maybe she's dreaming about Mamma's long arms, arms that unfurl and wrap themselves around her and lift her up to heaven.

When I was little, before I learned how to kill the beast in the forest, I used to have dreams like that, too.

Corinne

I asked Martin, "You have two children?"

"Stella has two children," he said. "I have one. Amanda isn't mine. But as far as I know Bee is mine, yes."

"As far as I know Bee is mine," I echoed. "What makes you put it like that?"

Martin did not answer. We sat on either side of the dining table, and neither of us said a thing. I knew if I waited long enough he wouldn't be able to stand the silence.

"I don't know what it is with Bee," he said, after a while.

"She was born less than a year after you moved in with Stella?"

"She was conceived at Høylandet," he replied. "We were there just after we met, for Harriet's—my grandmother's—birthday party."

"Were you happy when Stella told you she was pregnant?"

"I thought she grew more and more beautiful with each month that passed. Stella was exceptionally tall and now she was also exceptionally big. She was two and I was one. I looked at her and she was two. She was Bee and she was Stella, and with them I could find rest."

"You already knew she was going to be called Bee?"

"Yes and no. We had decided to name her after my Swedish

great-grandmother, Beatrice. We knew we were going to call her Bea—b-e-a—short for Beatrice. And we knew she had been conceived at Høylandet. At night I used to lie with my head on Stella's stomach and tell the baby all the wonderful stories I could think of. I could picture her, almost walking out of her mother, a perfect little creature, a perfect little face. Sometimes we called her Bea. Sometimes we called her Herr Poppel."

"But you said, 'Yes and no?'"

"Yeah, well, you see, when it came to it she was never a Beatrice, or a Bea with a b-e-a, she was just Bee."

Martin paused for a moment, seemingly deep in thought. He lit a cigarette. "Those were good times."

"Good times for both of you? Stella was never unwell during her pregnancy?"

"No, she was never unwell."

"And Stella's other daughter, Amanda, how did she take all this? She must have been around five when Stella got pregnant."

"Something like that, yes. I don't know. Amanda and I have never been close. I'll be honest with you. Amanda was—how shall I put it?—Amanda was in the way, Amanda was—"

"—never anyone's favorite," I murmured.

"Sorry?" Martin looked puzzled.

"I said, Amanda was never anyone's favorite. I beg your pardon. It annoys the life out of the guys on the squad, too, my finishing other people's sentences. Bad habit!"

Martin looked at me. Then he said, "Amanda had nothing to do with Stella and me. Now and then I might have acted as though I was fond of her. It was important for Stella that I should be fond of her. I would take her on my lap, but she always wriggled free. I couldn't do it, this father thing, with Amanda. She annoyed me. She was in the way."

"How exactly was she in the way?"

"We had a lot of fun together back then. Playing."

"Playing? What do you mean? Who was playing?"

"Stella and I," he replied. "We played games. We'd meet at

supermarkets and pretend we didn't know each other. We'd each take a basket and wander around the store, flirting with strangers, stealing a pack of spaghetti, juggling with apples, doing a little dance with the brooms, and so on, until one of us, usually Stella, burst out laughing. Which meant that I had won."

"You had won."

"I had won. One day I got into an argument with the checkout lady because she insisted that a cauliflower is a cauliflower."

"I see. . . ."

"Stella was standing in line behind me. We acted as if we didn't know each other. We'd made a deal beforehand that neither of us was allowed to use a basket or a cart. We'd collected as much as we could manage to carry in our arms, and then some. . . . Okay, so there she was in line right behind me, very pregnant, her arms laden with milk, bread, fish fingers, meatballs, soap powder, potatoes, apples, oatmeal, and lightbulbs, her face getting redder and redder. I remember thinking that she looked close to collapse—and then I got into this discussion with the woman at the register as to whether a cauliflower really was a cauliflower."

I asked Martin, "So in your eyes a cauliflower is not a cauliflower?"

"I maintained, for the sake of argument, that cauliflower was broccoli and broccoli was cauliflower," he answered. "Just to annoy the people behind me in line—other people's contempt is so easily aroused, other people's aggression—and to see how long Stella could last behind me."

"With her arms full."

"With her arms full, right. So I was standing there, pointing at the receipt, which stated that I had purchased five heads of cauliflower, and insisting that I had purchased five heads of broccoli. The checkout lady sighed and said that, in any case, cauliflower—which was on special—cost the same as broccoli, so it really didn't make any difference what you called it, at which I shook my head and said, 'Makes no difference? Makes no difference? Fair's fair! If I buy broccoli, then as far as I'm concerned, broccoli is what it should say right here, and if I buy cauliflower, then it should say cauliflower.' The line was starting to get restless; I could hear muttering behind me and the odd groan. Stella butted me with her enormous belly, I could feel the tip of her navel against my back, as if to tell me *enough is enough,* and a man farther down the line yelled, 'Come on, cut the crap!' I pulled myself up to my full height and said again, 'Fair's fair. I refuse to accept a receipt that states I have purchased something I have not purchased.' The checkout lady heaved another great sigh and pulled out a folder from under the register. It contained pictures of all the different vegetables in the world. Triumphantly she located the picture of cauliflower, with the word CAULI-FLOWER written in block letters underneath it. I looked at the picture. I looked at the letters. A hush fell around me. I could feel Stella's breath on the back of my neck. 'Martin, give it up, please, the joke's over.'

"'No,' I said at last. 'Fair's fair!'

"'No?' the checkout lady repeated, flabbergasted.

"'No!' I said firmly. 'It's wrong. The book's wrong, you're wrong, everybody's wrong. This is a crazy, crazy world.' I pulled a cauliflower out of my bag, held it up in front of me like a skull, and announced, 'This is broccoli!'"

"And then what happened?"

"Well, then a lot of things happened at once," Martin said. "First there was this almighty groan, a collective groan, the unmistakable sound of tempers snapping. A young man from the back of the line charged up to the front and made a dive at me with both fists clenched. The checkout lady broke into hysterical laughter. And Stella dropped her armful of shopping on the floor. When she did, a lady came running over to her, crying, '*Oh, my dear . . . oh, look at you . . . here, let me help you.*' Everyone went quiet. Stella was sitting on the floor, her legs stretched straight out, in a puddle of water, surrounded by groceries. Even the man who was about to lay into me had gone quiet, stopped in his tracks, his face turned to Stella, his fist still in midair. Stella's eyes met mine. 'It's Bea,' she whispered. 'Bea's on the way.' She looked all around, meeting the eyes of the others in the line. 'Look at the mess I've made . . . I'm sorry . . . water every-where . . . Martin, can you get the car?'

"Then: '*Now* will you stop it?' she pleaded. 'This game, I mean?'

"'Yes, of course.' I dropped to the floor beside her, put my arms around her, and we both started to giggle. The other people in line didn't know what to think. Some of them laughed, others shook their heads, and the nice woman who had come to Stella's aid picked the groceries up off the floor and put them in a basket. I got to my feet and thanked her. A little man, over seventy if he was a day, with not a hair on his head or his face and with tiny gnarled hands, bent gingerly over Stella, who was still on the floor, and asked if she really did know me or whether she was just a bit confused, due to the circumstances. He pointed to the puddle of water. She said, yes, of course she knew me. 'So you were standing right behind him in line while he was going on and on, insisting that cauliflower was broccoli, and you never said a single word?' he asked. Yes, she said, she supposed she was. And then the man crouched down and whispered in her ear, 'I hope, for your sake, that you know what you're giving birth to today!' The man pointed his right index finger at Stella's stomach. '*Wretched little thing*,' he said. '*Wretched little creature.*' Then he stood up and walked off."

Martin removed another cigarette from his pack but did not light it. Instead, he sat there fiddling with it.

"That's when Stella screamed," he said at last.

"Stella screamed?" I said.

"Yes, she screamed. She was screaming at the old man, screaming that he was an evil old man, that he had no right to say things like that, that he should come back this minute and beg the unborn child's forgiveness, that for all he knew she could be carrying an angel. But the man, who by this time was on his way out of the store, just shook his head and disappeared through the door with his shopping bag. I did my best to calm her down. The whole place was in an uproar. She was crying and screaming. Screaming at me to make that man come back here, screaming that he had to beg Bea's forgiveness. But she had gone into labor. I couldn't worry about him. We had to get to the hospital; there was no time to lose."

Amanda

When Bee was born, at first I thought she was really strange, because she never cried and because she had big eyes, like a cat. But Bee's not strange.

The old geezer showed me a magic trick once; he made this little doll all dressed in red disappear before my eyes. It was one of those old-fashioned dolls with big blue eyes and long eyelashes and red lips that open and say *Ma-ma*. I asked him if he could do the same thing with people, get them to disappear like that. He thought I meant Bee. He thought I wanted Bee to disappear. He said it was normal for children to be jealous of their little brothers or sisters. He had felt like killing his own little sister when he was a boy, a long time ago. But that wasn't what I meant. I was wondering whether he could make *me* disappear, because I wanted to be where the vanished people are, to see what it's like there, to round that world.

Corinne

"I had a dream right after Bee was born," Martin said. "A bloody clump on the operating table, a shapeless living thing, frail and exhausted, a thing that was dying but still breathing, and Stella was crying and saying, 'But we can save her, Martin, we can save her!' And when the clump pulls itself up, when the clump stops being a clump, Stella shouts at me to take her in my arms so she won't fall and hurt herself."

Martin lit a cigarette.

"I never used to dream before Bee was born. Stella said, 'Of course you dream at night, Martin, you just don't remember. Everybody dreams,' said Stella. But I was sure I had never dreamt before. I had slept soundly every night, and if scenes were being played out in my mind's eye, I certainly wasn't aware of it. My nights were still and blue."

"But then Bee came into the world, and the very first night after she was born you had a dream about her, right?"

"A horrible dream. A bloody clump, half alive, half dead, pulling itself up."

And it didn't stop there. The next night he had another dream. This time he dreamt about Bee's eyes. Bee was all eyes, eyes that were far too big. He had fathered a baby with eyes that were far too big, far too round, the eyes of a beast of prey. And so it went. Every night he dreamt about the child, and every dream was worse than the one before. Bee came to him in his sleep in a succession of different guises. She was disgusting things that he had spat out or with which he had fouled the street, she was battered, abused, covered in bruises and sores.

Sometimes in his dreams he was abusing her, lying on top of her in her bassinet. She was all eyes.

She was all eyes, and yet she was always Bee.

"She was Bee, born of woman, not quite a month old, and yet," says Martin, "and yet. . . ."

He showed me photographs of Bee from those first weeks. Martin was not the type to whip out the family pictures every chance he got, so it was me who asked.

"Did you take any photographs?" I asked.

"I didn't, but Stella did," he said.

I bowed my head over pictures of Bee. In her bassinet; on the floor at the moment she lifted her head for the first time; on the changing table enveloped in a red towel. Exceptionally big eyes, yes, there was no getting away from it, but otherwise, as far as I could see, just another pink-and-white baby girl.

"I woke up every morning with these images, these pictures in my head," Martin told me. "Not the photographs you're looking at here, but night pictures I was powerless to ward off. She'd be lying in her bassinet in our room, and Stella would get up to hold her, though she didn't cry much. People told us we were lucky to have a baby who never cried. Stella would get up and put Bee to her breast. 'Look at her,' Stella would say. 'Look how she feeds.' But the pictures were still there. I mean, she was lying right there, I could see that, I could accept that, a helpless little creature sucking at her mother's breast, and it would be light outside, I'd hear that it was morning, hear someone slamming a car door or calling to a dog. You'd think I could have stroked the back of that soft, furrowed infant neck or taken one of those tiny hands in my big one. But no! Because night after night I was haunted by this child. This alien child. This alien child. She was so alien; do you know what I mean?"

I nodded.

"Of course Stella noticed that I wouldn't touch our baby. That I turned away every time she came toward me with Bee in her arms. To begin with she was furious. 'What is your problem?' she'd scream. 'What kind of way is this to behave?' 'Give me time,' I'd say. I told her I was jealous, that the baby took up all her attention and there was none left for me. She'd shake her head and stalk out of the room. But after a while she retreated into herself. The sound of her crying would reach me in every room. I'd go to her and put my arms around her. 'What's the matter with you?' she'd say. 'Don't you love her?' 'Of course I love her,' I'd say. 'Of course I do, Stella.' I'd work myself up into a temper. 'Of course I do! Do you think you're the only one who knows how to love a child? Is yours the only love that's good enough?' I'd yell at her, even though I knew how hollow it sounded. She would yell back that it was hard to believe a man loved his own child when he couldn't even touch her. And after a while she began to challenge me. She turned nasty—that's the only way to put it. In the blink of an eye, Stella could turn downright nasty. I would see it in her face, the little smile twisting her lips, a hand brushed swiftly through her hair, her accusing—no, mocking—eyes.

"We'd be sitting at the dinner table, Amanda, Stella, and me, this table here," and Martin thumped the table. "Stella would be sitting where you're sitting. I'd be sitting here. Amanda would be over there. Bee would be in her bassinet in the bedroom, but sometimes we'd hear her grunt. Even though she never really cried, she did make some sounds. Stella would keep on eating. Bee would grunt louder. Grunt is the wrong word, though. She whimpered. Yes, that's it. She whimpered. And Stella would go on eating.

"Amanda would say, 'Mamma, Bee's crying.'

"Stella would say, 'Yes, so she is.'

"Then Amanda would ask, 'Should I go get her?'

"And Stella would say, 'Martin should get Bee.' Then she would add softly, 'Thanks, Amanda, you're a good big sister, but it's Martin's turn to get Bee.'

"So I would get up and go to the bedroom to get Bee. Lift her out of her bassinet, walk back to the dining room, and hand her to Stella.

"And the dreams continued. Sometimes I would get it into my head that the baby was evil. That this baby was, in fact, willfully haunting me. I grew convinced that Stella had given birth to some evil thing.

"It became more and more difficult to deny Stella's accusations, silent though they were, now. We'd been looking forward to this, she and I, to Bee, little Bee, named after my great-grandmother with the ostrich-feather hat.

"To make amends I tried to devote myself to my stepdaughter instead. I tried to get closer to Amanda. I took her to the movies, picked her up from school, attended PTA meetings. For her seventh birthday I took her to Copenhagen. We went to Tivoli Gardens and ate popcorn and cotton candy. I had managed to persuade Stella not to come with us, to stay at home and take it easy with Bee.

"'We all need a bit of time,' I said, tugging Amanda's hair. 'Time together and time apart. Amanda and I will manage just fine without you two for a couple of days.' This said in a gently teasing, tender manner. Stella, happy that I was at last taking an interest in Amanda but disappointed, nonetheless, that things still weren't working out with Bee, merely nodded and smiled. Amanda hissed at me not to tug her hair.

"Afterward, when Stella was out of earshot, Amanda turned her face up at me and said, 'We're not friends, you and I, and don't you forget it!'

"'No, no, of course not,' I said, somewhat taken aback, although in my heart of hearts I felt the same way. And then I said, 'So why do you want to go to Copenhagen with me for your birthday?'

"'Because I want to go to Tivoli,' Amanda said. 'I want to ride the Ferris wheel.'

"And that was that. We went to Copenhagen. We celebrated her birthday in true time-honored fashion. We went to Tivoli. We rode the Ferris wheel. And best of all, in the hotel room that first night, in the narrow bed next to Amanda's narrow bed, I slept. And I slept. A sleep without dreams. A sleep with no pictures. And the night after that, too, and the night after that. Three nights in a hotel in Copenhagen with no dreams of any sort, the pictures in my mind's eye faded away, and I thought, Now I can go home to Stella and Bee and put my arms around them both and tell them that I love them."

When Martin and Amanda got back from Copenhagen, Martin walked straight into the bedroom, where Stella was lying asleep with Bee. He hugged them both. Later that evening, he gave Bee her bath, lowering her into the lukewarm water, filling his cupped hand with water, and trickling it gently over her head. He did this several times, filled his cupped hand with water and trickled it over her head, until she actually smiled. She's smiling at me, he said to himself. You're smiling at me. He lifted her out of the tub, laid her on the changing table, and wrapped her in a big red towel. Two huge eyes gazed at him with wonder, and he gazed back with wonder every bit as great.

But that same night the dreams returned, and he was jolted awake.

He reached out for Stella, but Bee was lying between them. Bee was awake. She stared at him. He stared back. It's not normal for babies to stare like that, he thought. Babies howl and drool and laugh and suck, but they're not supposed to stare! Martin lifted the eiderdown as if he fully expected to find a coiled serpent under there instead of a baby's body. Bee was naked except for a diaper full of poop. He picked her up and laid her in her bassinet. She whimpered. He put a finger to her lips: "Ssh." She whimpered again. He pressed his finger against her lips. "Ssh! I said. Go to sleep!" At last he turned away, grabbed a pillow, and went off to lie down on the sofa in the living room.

Stella woke up and called him. He heard her pad over to the bassinet and take Bee in her arms, heard the words she said.

Sweet, gentle words, I imagine, words murmured to a child in the middle of the night.

Video Recording: Stella & Martin
The House by the Lady Falls
8/27/00, 4:30 A.M.

MARTIN: Everything of value. How exactly would you
            define that, Stella?

STELLA: I knew this substitute teacher once, in sixth or
            seventh grade. She was actually a dressmaker, but
            the dresses she made didn't pay the rent, so she
            substituted at school. She used to ask me if I'd like
            to go for a walk after class. She wasn't particularly
            good-looking, short and plump, but she had nice
            eyes that really saw me. She said, "Stella, you're
            tall, you play the flute well, you have five fingers on
            each hand, you can be whatever you want to be.
            There is no end to you. You have unlimited
            depths." Her name was Frederikke Moll. I
            remember, because I used to say her name over and
            over again inside my head. Frederikke Moll.
            Frederikke Moll.

MARTIN: Why are you telling me this now?

STELLA: Because you started babbling about "everything of
            value," and this is a memory I value.

Stella Descending

MARTIN: But we're talking about things here, Stella, not
memories. Everything of value, said that most
excellent insurance broker Gunnar R. Owesen, and
off he went. Everything of value. Every thing's
value. The sofa. The glass table. The candlesticks.
The flower vases. The bookcases and the books.
Nothing of value, really. The photographs on the
wall. What else? The silver, did you say? Okay!
Passing through the living room and into the
dining room. Eight red chairs, one large dark
dining table, a picture on the wall of a red sun
sinking into a black sea, another picture, of a
puddle on tarmac, welcome to our home, and on we
go. Look! This lovely room painted blue is the
kitchen. Do you think Mr. Insurance Broker
Gunnar R. Owesen and his colleagues sit and
watch these videos, Stella? This documentation of
rooms and things? Should we open the cupboards?
Should we open the drawers? Now, what have we
here? A perfect mess! A potato peeler, a corkscrew,
a pencil sharpener, an Easter chick, a receipt for
something, an unsent letter from Stella to Axel
Grutt, three unopened bills, a broken knife, an old
drawing of Amanda's depicting, not surprisingly, a
red house that also happens to be some sort of
ferocious monster—wouldn't you say, Stella? And
what would the child psychologists say if they
could see your daughter's drawings? A pack of PP
pastilles—you can't buy them anywhere these
days—three pot holders, a bunch of keys, a copy of
a tax return from . . . let's see . . . three years ago, a
collection of poems by e. e. cummings. Nope! Back
into the drawer, all of it. Nothing of value here.

STELLA: Try the third drawer to the right.

MARTIN: Third drawer to the right it is!

STELLA: D'you see anything?

MARTIN: Do I ever! All glittering and gleaming.

STELLA: No it isn't, Martin. I doubt if it's glittering *or* gleaming. It hasn't glittered and gleamed since we polished it two years ago. I believe the first and last time we ever got that silverware out was for Bee's seventh birthday.

MARTIN: Dear little Bee.

STELLA: And what's that supposed to mean?

MARTIN: It means I can just picture her sitting at the table eating, with those shaky scab-encrusted hands of hers, or lying in bed, asleep and panting as if she were on the run, even in her sleep. I don't know what else to say, Stella, except *dear little Bee.*

STELLA: You say it with such a . . . such a note of contempt in your voice—dear little Bee, like that—I can't help wondering whether you mean it.

MARTIN: Mean what?

STELLA: That word *dear.* Whether your daughter is . . . well . . . *dear* to you.

MARTIN: Your body, Stella, is dear to me, and everything that issues from your body—all the sighs, groans, words, tears, laughter, excrement, blood, vomit, discharges, kids, the one that isn't mine and the other one that is—I love it, all of it.

STELLA: I was trying to talk to you, Martin. Seriously. It's all a joke to you, isn't it, even when we're talking

about our child. Put that camera down! I've got
something to tell you!

MARTIN: All a joke. Stella wants to be serious. But I'm not
going to put the camera down. We've got stuff to
do. We're supposed to be talking about things, not
children. Gunnar R. Owesen isn't interested in our
children; he probably has a whole fucking houseful
of kids himself. But precious objects, on the other
hand! Gold and silver! These he wants to hear
more about. . . . Let's see, now. Nine big forks. Nine
small forks. Nine big knives. Nine small knives.
Ten tablespoons.

STELLA: They're soupspoons.

MARTIN: I beg your pardon, soupspoons! Ten soupspoons.
Ten teaspoons. Maybe we should explain to the
insurance broker why we have nine of some things
and ten of others and a complete dozen of nothing.
Take the camera for a minute, Stella, and I'll
explain. Can you see me?

STELLA: I've got you in close-up, Martin.

MARTIN: What do you see?

STELLA: Your face, your eyes.

MARTIN: Let me explain about the silver forks, the silver
knives, and the silver spoons. They were a gift
from Stella's mother, my mother-in-law, the lady
whose stomach never rumbled, not till she was
lying on her deathbed. Isn't that right, Stella?

STELLA: Well, yes. But have some respect for the dead,
please.

MARTIN: Why the dead more than the living?

STELLA: Because they can't defend themselves.

MARTIN: And you think the living can?

STELLA: No, that's not what I think—

MARTIN: The fact is, Stella's mother, whose stomach never rumbled till she was lying on her deathbed, felt we ought to have some silverware in our drawer. She was quite a lady, was Stella's mother.

STELLA: She was not a lady, she was a tree.

MARTIN: Come again, Stella?

STELLA: Mamma wanted to be a tree. When I was little, I once asked her, Why are you always so quiet, Mamma? To which she replied, Because I want to be as quiet as a tree. And I said, What sort of tree? And Mamma said, It makes no difference.

MARTIN: Nevertheless, it would have been a fine tree. Not a fir tree, at any rate.

STELLA: Maybe a Siberian weeping birch.

MARTIN: No, not her. You're a Siberian weeping birch, Stella. Not your mother. She was a cherry tree.

STELLA: Who gave us gifts of silverware.

MARTIN: Exactly. Every Christmas we were presented with more silver. She had a system, too. I like that. A regular system. Everyone should have a system. It went like this: On Stella's birthdays she gave us knives. On my birthdays she gave us forks. For Christmas she gave us spoons. What is Stella's mother actually thinking here? She's thinking, Stella is a knife, so I'll give her knives. Which is, in fact, very apt, seeing as Stella actually sleeps with a knife under her pillow, in case the beast should come to get her. And I am a fork. Martin is a fork, Stella's mother thinks. Look at that silver fork there, get a really good shot of that silver fork, Stella, a close-up, so Mr. Gunnar R. Owesen, insurance broker, can gaze upon it in all its splendor. That fork has something in common with me—okay, now turn the camera on me, Stella—but I don't know what it is. I don't know what it is I have in common with a fork. Why did Stella's mother give me forks for my birthday every year?

STELLA: Maybe because forks are jagged.

MARTIN: Or five-fingered.

STELLA: They're called tines, Martin. And there are only four.

MARTIN: Forks are too straight for my liking.

STELLA: But unlike knives they split at the tip.

MARTIN: Which brings us to the spoons. Because every Christmas Eve, Stella and I received a joint present from Stella's mother. One teaspoon and one soup-spoon. Look at this spoon. A close-up of the spoon, Stella! I've chosen the soupspoon. I prefer the soupspoon to the teaspoon. The teaspoon is ditzy. The teaspoon is a poodle, a pocket mirror, a skinny straitlaced woman. The soupspoon, on the other hand, is all rounded and soft and nice and, unlike knives and forks, it's not dangerous to put in your mouth. The soupspoon reminds me of you curled up against me and me curled up against you at night. . . . Anyway, that was the story of the nine knives and the nine forks and the ten spoons. Un-fortunately, Stella's mother died around Christmastime a year ago. She just managed to give us the tenth teaspoon and the tenth soupspoon before drawing her last breath and ascending to heaven.

STELLA: Martin, would you take the camera now?

MARTIN: Okay.

STELLA: I want you to come over here.

MARTIN: Over where?

STELLA: Into the hall. I want you to get a shot of this. Because from a purely objective point of view, it actually is valuable.

MARTIN: I think it's hideous, Stella.

STELLA: It is not. It's lovely.

MARTIN: A stuffed female torso draped in an old pink lace dress. Hideous!

STELLA: It's a dressmaker's dummy, Martin. I want you to get a shot of it. You shoot it and I'll do the talking.

MARTIN: I'll shoot and you'll do the talking.

STELLA: I want to say something about this lace dress. Can you shut up for one minute?

MARTIN: By all means. I shoot, you talk, right? Okay, Stella, fire away!

STELLA: Thank you, Martin. . . . The pink lace dress you see hanging here was left to me by my mother—

MARTIN: Who gave birth to my darling Stella without feeling any pain. She did not feel the slightest twinge of pain, Stella's mother, my mother-in-law, whose stomach never rumbled till she was lying on her deathbed.

Stella Descending

STELLA: You're interrupting again!

MARTIN: Sorry, Stella. But I think the insurance broker
            ought to hear this story. Picture her if you will, Mr.
            Gunnar R. Owesen: Long-haired Edith Lind,
            Stella's mother, my mother-in-law, whose stomach
            never rumbled till she was lying on her deathbed,
            sitting on a windowsill in the maternity ward,
            reading a book. The contractions are coming at
            two-minute intervals, and later at one-minute
            intervals. There is little doubt that she is in the last
            stages of labor. And yet there is nothing about
            Edith's actions, her facial expression, or her voice
            to indicate that she is in pain. Occasionally the
            midwife has to ask her to put down her book so she
            can listen to her stomach. The baby's heartbeat is
            rapid and strong, but the midwife can hear other
            sounds, too. What is it with this child? she thinks.
            What kind of noises is it making, there in its
            mother's womb? You may think, Gunnar R.
            Owesen, that all the midwife can hear when she
            listens at the mother's stomach is the baby's
            heartbeat. Not so. The midwife can hear all sorts of
            noises. Sometimes she hears sighs, gurgles,
            whispers, laughter, whistling, at other times
            something that sounds like shouts, from children
            who don't wish to be born, perhaps. And this time
            she hears sounds not unlike crying, not unlike
            screams, right, Stella?

STELLA: Right.

MARTIN: After the midwife has listened to her stomach,
            long-haired Edith Lind, my mother-in-law, whose
            stomach never rumbled till she was lying on her
            deathbed, reads a verse out loud. And the midwife

will remember that verse for a long time, to this very day, in fact, because Edith reads it several times, in a soft singing voice, a very beautiful voice. The midwife, that splendid old woman, thinks to herself that all women have their own way of bidding a new baby welcome, and this is Edith Lind's way. To read or to sing, because it is as if she is singing when she reads, a verse about love. But that's not the case, is it, Stella? The midwife is mistaken. It's not you Edith Lind is thinking of when she sings. It's not you. She doesn't even feel pain; she feels no more pain than that stuffed torso over there; her face doesn't change color when the contractions surge through her body, she turns neither red nor white, she is just as pale and composed as the lace dress. Does she feel anything at all? Well, possibly a restless sense of discomfort at being there. She would much rather be somewhere else . . . so she sings. How does that Swedish song go again?

STELLA: *I pull her golden locks . . .*

MARTIN: *Is it you, O impossible one?*

STELLA: *Is it you?*

MARTIN: *Bewildered I gaze into her face . . .*

STELLA: *Are the gods, then, playing with us?*

MARTIN: Eventually the midwife has to ask Edith to settle herself in the birthing chair, but she doesn't want to. She wants to stand. So Edith stands bolt upright on the floor, clinging to a young nurse who has come in to assist and who is soon to have her young life ruined by your arrival, Stella. The midwife hunkers down in front of Edith, preparing to catch the child. And she can see inside Edith now, up into her, way up inside her, and what she sees is big and red and wet, that's you, Stella, and you're screaming even before you come into the world. You fall down through Edith's birth canal, fall into the world, fall into the splendid old midwife's splendid old hands; you fall wide-eyed, long and slender, like a diver from a cliff—but with an unearthly scream that bursts the young nurse's eardrum, with the result that today, thirty-five years later, she is still deaf in the left ear.

STELLA: She's gone deaf in the right ear, too.

MARTIN: Well, I'll be. . . . How did you know that?

STELLA: I met her through my work. At a conference. Her name is Alma Blom. She's over sixty now. When I introduced myself, she asked if I was Edith Lind's daughter, and when I said yes, she realized who I was and we had quite a long chat. I knew my mother had kept in touch with her for years after I was born, had sent her letters and sometimes even money, in compensation for the damage to her ear. Alma confirmed all this. She confirmed that my mother seemed to feel no pain during labor, that she sang of love during the contractions, and that she left the hospital that same day, just a few hours after I was born, with me wrapped in a pink blanket. Oh, and of course she confirmed that I burst her eardrum the moment I fell into the world.

MARTIN: And what did you say to that?

STELLA: I said I was sorry.

MARTIN: And what did she say?

STELLA: She said you can't blame a child for the things she does before she's even a minute old. Besides which, she'd gone deaf in the right ear, too.

MARTIN: Another baby?

STELLA: No. She gave up obstetrics after the incident with me and switched to working with cancer patients instead—in other words, we're colleagues. I don't know why she went deaf in her right ear. But she can read lips and she speaks clearly, so carrying on a conversation with her is no problem at all.

MARTIN: Take a good look at this dressmaker's dummy, take a good look at this lace dress. The dress is old. An antique. How much do you think it's worth, Stella?

STELLA: I've no idea.

MARTIN: She has no idea. We'll need to find out what it's worth. A good few thousand kroner, I'd imagine. Stella inherited it from her mother, and it was a present to Stella's mother from a lady by the name of Ella. You see, Mr. Gunnar R. Owesen, even though Stella and I have never met Ella, she is a part of our life, so she figures in our conversation. Ella was, by all accounts, the only person in the world ever to hear long-haired Edith Lind, Stella's mother, my mother-in-law, whose stomach never rumbled till she was lying on her deathbed, cry out loud. Make any sound at all. You know the sort of sounds I'm talking about, don't you, Owesen? Laughter, Owesen. Moans of desire. Have you ever heard a naked woman burp with pleasure? Edith Lind left her husband and her little daughter as often as she could to be with Ella, and when she came home, the only signs that she had been cheating on her husband were flushed cheeks and an extra dash of pepper on her dinner. Stella has a photograph of her mother's lover. She found it in one of her father's desk drawers when he died. An elegant, fair-haired, plump woman, around forty-five in this picture, although they had been lovers for many years before it was taken. How many years, Stella?

STELLA: Twenty years.

MARTIN: Twenty years. All those years when you were growing up, they were lovers. She's dead now, Ella is. They're all dead now. Stella's mother, Ella, and Stella's father. Stella's the only one left. Her and her kids.

STELLA: I wish you wouldn't say it like that.

MARTIN: Like what?

STELLA: The way you said it. *Stella's the only one left. Her and her kids.*

MARTIN: But it's true, isn't it?

STELLA: You know what I think, Martin? I think the difference between you and me, and what makes you sometimes such a pain in the ass and so cold, is that you were loved as a child. It's made you spoiled and inconsiderate.

MARTIN: What in the world? Where did all this anger come from?

STELLA: Good night, Martin.

MARTIN: We're not done yet.

STELLA: We're done.

Corinne

"The nights were awful. Awful." Martin said, putting his head in his hands.

Outside it was dark, November dark, even though it was September and the heat of the last few days had been anything but autumnal. In the apartment all was quiet. If Martin had been talking louder, instead of telling his story in something close to a whisper, we would have heard the faint echo of his voice in that room with its remarkable acoustics.

"What makes you say that?" I asked him.

"Because nights with Stella were anything but good," he said.

"In what way, anything but good?" I said.

"We never slept."

"You never slept. Ever?"

"Never. I didn't want to sleep anymore. Bee was haunting me . . . this little baby . . . she did it on purpose, I'm sure of it, invaded my dreams, and it was getting so I hated her. My dreams were becoming more and more violent, more and more— how can I put it?—disgusting. In them I took off my clothes and jumped on her like an animal, entering her, fucking her, a baby, a deformed, abused, skinny, scabby baby—we were both deformed . . . one-legged, thirteen-fingered, dying things . . . in the end there was no knowing which was her and which was me . . . it was sick . . . and I'm not like that, you know? I'm not like that. It was just in these dreams. God, how I hated her! Not only at night but during the day too. This silent helpless little creature who never took her eyes off me and never behaved like other babies. And I couldn't tell any of this to Stella. She was the child's mother. I told her I had terrible nightmares, but not what they were about, just that I could no longer bear to sleep at night. I preferred to sleep during the day, when it was light, because then the pictures weren't as vivid. I switched jobs, gave up selling furniture for a while, took to working nights, stacking crates in a warehouse. I'd come home at four in the morning and wake Stella."

"What did you do for the rest of the night once you'd woken Stella?" I ask.

"We made up games to pass the time. We'd always played games anyway, daring each other to do things, telling each other stories, messing around. . . .

"During the day, Stella went to work, took care of the children, cooked dinner, went to PTA meetings, visited women friends and Axel Grutt—all while I was asleep. I no longer participated in the day-to-day side of our life together. Not that I lay in bed and slept all day, that's not what I mean; we ate our meals together, we dealt with the house, behaved like parents of a sort. Occasionally I might even take the girls into town or to the movies or help them with their homework. The years passed, and Bee got bigger. But to me she was still repulsive. When I went anywhere with children, I would make a point of holding Amanda's hand, not Bee's, and when Amanda got so big she wouldn't hold my hand anymore, I told her she should at least hold her sister's hand, so she wouldn't get lost, although the truth is I had this fantasy that she *would* get lost and never come back, find a gingerbread house in the woods. But I became expert at hiding all this, and Stella was happy to see me getting involved with the kids—thinking up fun things to do with them, taking an interest in their welfare, kissing Bee in the presence of witnesses. Kissing Amanda cost me nothing, but then Amanda had always pulled away from me.

"Like I said, I didn't sleep all day, even though I worked nights, but I went through the motions, in my sleep as it were; taking in the day's events much, I guess, as other people would take in some crazy dream: like a succession of abstract, often disjointed pictures that had both something and nothing to do with me. When evening came I would liven up. I went to work, and Stella went to bed early.

"Eventually it reached the point where we lived—talked, fucked, and played—at night, in the hours between three and six—"

Martin broke off, got up from his chair, and left the room.

"I just have to get something," he called back, and I heard his footsteps going up the stairs to the second floor and the three bedrooms: Stella and Martin's room, Amanda's room, Bee's room. Moments later he returned. In his hands he had a large black blanket or shawl.

"This shawl hung over the window in the bedroom to block out the morning light," he said. "It began with this shawl, our nighttime games. How many years ago I couldn't say, it must have been spring or summertime, Bee would have been about three, or maybe four. At any rate it was a nuisance, its being so warm and light outside both day and night, so Stella found this shawl in the attic and hung it over the window. I came home as usual around three or four in the morning and climbed into bed beside her. Then we lay there hand in hand, perfectly still, and watched the morning light gradually filtering in through the dark fabric, which was more worn in some places than others. Stella said, 'Look at the woman on the shawl.' 'What woman?' I said. 'The woman bending down to pick a child up off the grass,' she said. And then I saw it, the outline of a flickering magic-lantern slide: a woman bending down to pick a child up off the grass. But then the woman turned into a car driving flat out along a deserted freeway in the middle of the night. I told Stella that the woman had turned into a car driving flat out along a deserted freeway in the middle of the night, and she said that the freeway was actually a skyscraper, or a tower, and on the top of the skyscraper or tower was a tightrope walker, standing on one leg, singing. Yeah—and so it went on. We started up our own all-night picture show . . . and one night Stella said—or maybe it was me who said it—that the pictures might be trying to tell us something."

Martin ran a hand over the shawl before giving it to me.

"To lie in bed at night and look at the black shawl over the window was a little like lying in the grass and looking at the clouds. Pictures would start to form. Faces. Nice or nasty, depending."

(III)

FALL

Stella

Sometimes when I'm with you, Axel, when I come to visit you, I look at myself in the gilt mirror in the hall. Then I imagine that you come to stand behind me and that it is your face I see. You are old and ugly and I love you. But I don't like it when you touch me. I find it repulsive. Your hands are cold. You won't let go of me when I'm ready to leave.

IT IS NIGHT. Martin is curled up in a ball in the middle of our big double bed, naked, skinny. Fists clenched, eyes squeezed tight shut, one arm covering his face as if he were warding off a blow. Or else he is sitting on the sofa in the living room, with the camera trained on the door, waiting for me to come back down and pick up where we left off.

I look at my face in the mirror.

During the day it's not so easy to detect all the tension, or fear, or anger that is written so large on Martin's face when he is asleep. I can see it, of course. After all the years we have lived together—of course I can see it. If I go right up close to him, feel his breath on my face, I can see it. If, instead of kissing him, I run my fingers over his lips, which are tight and hard and closed, I can feel it. If I start to count the tiny, almost invisible lines around his mouth, which he can no longer explain away. . . .

I have a photographic memory. I remember in pictures. Martin's face figures in so many of them, and in each picture there is another tight line around his mouth. He told me once that the reason we found living together so painful was that we always saw one another in close-up.

And even now, after all that's been said and done, there's no rest to be had. I'm sure that if he were to open his eyes now, he would see me standing here watching him. He would see that I am still very close by.

EVEN AS A CHILD I had trouble sleeping. Every time I felt myself falling asleep, I would think, Ah, at last I'm going to sleep—and then, of course, I didn't. One day I told Mamma the reason I couldn't sleep at night was that every time I thought I was finally drifting off, I seemed to be jolted out of it and found myself wide awake instead. "Well, then, you'll just have to stop thinking that," said Mamma. "You'll have to stop thinking, Ah, at last I'm going to sleep."

But lying in bed at night thinking about how you're not going to think about something is just the same as thinking about it—and I remained sleepless.

"Think of something else, then," said Mamma, who also couldn't sleep at night. I inherited my sleeplessness from her. I'm happy to have inherited *something* of hers, although I wish I had inherited something other than insomnia—her beautiful hair, for example, or her hands. But I'm glad there is some proof that I am her daughter, a bond between us.

I never dared to get up when I couldn't sleep. Which is how it came about that, when I was still just a child, I began to picture myself walking from room to room to look at the people I lived with. Pappa was not much to look at, not even in the imagination. He lay flat in bed, a lean gray man, snoring, with his head on the pillow. Mamma was another matter. I didn't dare call out to her, even though I knew she was awake. Mamma got so angry—a tight-lipped sort of anger, it was—if I bothered her as she sat, night after night, on the sofa with her legs tucked under her, staring out the big window in the living room.

"What are you thinking, Mamma?"
 No reply.
 "What are you thinking?"
 Mamma is like Bee. I look at her face, alien, impenetrable, hostile, like a landscape that is far too cold or far too hot, and I cannot imagine that we once shared the same body. I lay inside Mamma, and Bee lay inside me, but if I were to think of the three of us as an object of some sort, it would have to be a hatstand, with hooks sticking out in all directions.

When I think about Mamma, the first thing that comes to mind is her silence. As a little girl I often sit at the kitchen table in the afternoon. Mamma makes dinner, maybe, and I draw or do my homework. We live with Pappa in a new house with big square windows. It's winter; all the pictures from my early childhood are winter pictures. Sometimes I will stop whatever I am doing, put down my crayons or my books, hold my breath, not make a single sound, and look at Mamma standing by the kitchen window with a faraway look in her eyes, a cigarette between her fingers. All I can hear is the sound of her breathing. She makes no other sound—no sighing, no yawning, no swallowing or lip-smacking or humming or stomach rumblings, no rustling of clothes or jingling of bracelets. And this silence, Mamma's silence, not only reigns when she is standing by the kitchen window with a faraway look in her eyes, it reigns at all times. And it is not just she who is silent, but everything she does and everything she touches. I sit at the kitchen table, holding my breath and thinking that I, Stella, age nine, have an utterly silent mother. When she lights a cigarette, I don't hear the crackle of plastic being removed from the cigarette pack, no swoosh as she strikes a light on the side of the matchbox, no intake of breath from her lips as she takes the first puff. When she cooks dinner, I don't hear the usual chinking of pans, glass, and cutlery. And when we go to the store to buy food, I hear only my own feet trudging through the wet snow. I never really realized how silent Mamma was until I became aware of the sounds other women made. I remember one woman—a lady, really—who visited our school when I was in first grade. She had come to talk to us about how to use a toothbrush properly. She didn't look like a dentist. She didn't smell of fluoride. She didn't even wear a white coat, like the gruff old man in the basement—the school dentist—who was known as the Demon.

No, this strange lady wore a tight red dress. She had big breasts that made me think of balloons, and she smelled of some heady perfume. But above all, she made a lot of noises. Every time she lifted the big red toothbrush up to the huge flesh-colored plastic jaw with the twenty-eight chattering teeth—in order to demonstrate how we ought to brush—the four bracelets on her right wrist jingled and jangled. Her high stiletto heels beat out their own distinctive clickety-clack rhythm as she walked across the linoleum floor, and the tight red dress, which was made of some sort of shiny synthetic material, rustled if she so much as drew breath. She jingled and jangled and rattled and rustled—and each time the heavy gold ring on the second finger of her left hand struck the teacher's desk, it went *clunk, clunk, clunk.*

Eventually, silence becomes a blanket term for everything about Mamma: thin, flat-chested, clean, and reserved. Her cleanliness knows no bounds. Over and over again she turns on the faucet and washes her lovely long hands, scrupulously, with unscented soap. And over and over again she whispers to me that I must remember to bathe in the evening and shower in the morning. She never lets me see her naked, and—until the day she becomes terminally ill and is admitted to my ward—I am never able to think of Mamma as a seeping, odorous, rumbling, real-live body. She is an angel. Not a luminous angel with wings and long golden hair, but an angel nonetheless, with an angel's body and angel feet that always hover just above the ground.

At the age of thirteen I try to adopt Mamma's angelic appearance, without success. My body refuses to keep silent as hers does. My body bulges in all directions; it sweats and bleeds and shits. I can't control it. It will not obey me. I'm ashamed of it. Everywhere it goes my body draws attention to itself. It's so big, so conspicuous, always leaving some trace of itself behind. There go Stella and her body, *thumpity-thump*. There's no way of hiding it: the stink, the shit, the belly rumblings, the rash on my hands.

In my room I have a closet in which I hide stained sheets, panty hose, and panties. I know Mamma thinks I'm disgusting, but I don't want her to know *how* disgusting. Eventually the closet is so full I can't close the door properly, and at night, when I'm in bed, I can see the dark pile behind the door I cannot close threatening to spill out into the room.

As I say: I remember in pictures, photographs. A picture of Mamma at night, sitting on the sofa, legs tucked under her. A picture of Mamma standing by the kitchen window, faraway look in her eyes, cigarette between her fingers. In both pictures her face is turned away. I have other pictures too, but in all of them she has her face turned away. As a result, I don't recall her features all that well, her eyes, her mouth. I remember her hair, long and dark and shining. And I remember her hands, because they are beautiful and because sometimes she rubs my tummy when it aches. No other form of caress ever passes between us. Once, standing in the middle of the living room, I fling my arms around her waist, quite unprompted, and say, "Mamma!"

But I don't think she's too happy about this, even if she does give my hair a quick brush with her fingertips and whisper, "Stella . . . oh, Stella."

I don't have as many photographs of Pappa. Not in a waking state, at any rate. He sleeps a lot. At night, in the afternoon, and most certainly, as I am fond of imagining, during the day when he is at work. Pappa owns a gift shop in Oslo, where he sells all sorts of bric-a-brac. Behind the counter works an elderly lady called Miss Andersen; Pappa stays in the back room, keeping the books. I'm fond of imagining Pappa lying on the floor, surrounded by books, buried under a mound of books, sleeping the day away until it's time to catch the train home and carry on sleeping.

I have another picture of Pappa, almost the only one of him awake and in an upright position. We are alone in the house. Mamma is off somewhere. Sometimes she is just that: off somewhere. I never know where she is. She can be gone for a whole day and half the night too. Sometimes I can somehow hear she is back, or not exactly hear it but sense it. That she is in the house. That she is sitting on the sofa with her legs tucked under her. That the night is as it always is. But at this particular minute, on this particular day, Mamma is off somewhere, and both Pappa and I know for sure that she won't be back for hours, days maybe.

Pappa comes into my room with a laundry basket under his arm. He makes straight for the closet bulging with dirty sheets and stained underwear. I'm sitting on the bed. He pulls it all out, folds it, and lays it in the basket. Then he leaves the room. A little later, he pops his head round the door again and looks at me. His eyes are pale blue.

"Come on," he says. "We'll get all this washed before she comes home. She doesn't need to know anything about it. That's what I do: wait with things until she's not here. I mean, it's easier that way."

AXEL, AGAIN. There you are, waiting for me outside my hotel
in the middle of Copenhagen. It scared me, seeing you there. I
don't believe this is a coincidence. I believe you have actually followed me to Copenhagen. And there you are, on the street outside my hotel: courteous, false, ancient, and infatuated, telling
me you have business in Denmark. D'you want me to laugh out
loud? D'you want me to scream? What *do* you want? What do
you *want* with me?

For two days I've had to sit through lecture after lecture on
nursing the dying: pain relief, comfort, counseling, care. And
now here's the forever dying Axel Grutt, waiting for me outside
my hotel. And he won't be content with just going for coffee. He
wants to take me for a ride on a Ferris wheel.

A famous actress spoke to us about her son's death, a moving
story of white-clad nurses, cool hands, thin bandages, pain-
killing morphine, fluttering curtains. She kept repeating the
words *death with dignity, death with dignity, a truly beautiful death,*
while becoming tears rolled down her cheeks. When she finished, I asked if I might say a few words. I stepped up onto the
stage, stuck two fingers down my throat, and threw up. The

actress gasped, Oh, my God! I wiped my lips and asked for a glass of water.

"I'm afraid of heights," I tell Axel. "And besides, I'm a bit pushed for time."

"Afraid you might fall, or afraid you might jump?"

"Afraid I won't be able to get down again."

"I'll hold your hand."

Later, you tell me that you are related to the inventor of the Ferris wheel, an American engineer greater than Gustave Eiffel. Are you trying to impress me, Axel?

The worst thing about the Ferris wheel is not that it goes fast, because it doesn't; it moves with terrible slowness. The worst thing is that it stops when you get to the top, and there's no way of knowing when it will start to turn again.

THIS IS MY FIRST PICTURE of Martin. Imagine, if you will, a large bright room bare of furniture. The ceiling is high, and the wooden floor is worn. It could probably do with being sanded, but I like it as it is. I have one big window with fine, almost transparent pale-blue curtains, and in the center of the room is a new sofa. It's green. On the sofa sits Martin. He has had himself hoisted up the side of the building, has climbed in through the window, and now he's refusing to leave. He has set the sofa on the floor and himself on the sofa. He's laughing. He reaches his hand out to me. He says something or other, but the sound seems to get lost. I don't catch it, even though his lips are moving. The doorway in which I'm standing, between the bedroom and the living room, has a high sill that I always trip over on my way to bed at night.

I tell Martin, although I don't yet know his name is Martin, that I have to collect Amanda from nursery school. I tell him I would like him to leave. He has delivered the sofa and been paid, and now he has to leave.

"Are you sure I have to leave?" he asks.

"Yes," I say.

"The same way I came in, I suppose," he says, pointing to the window.

The crane, or hydraulic lift, or whatever it's called, the thing that carried Martin up to me, is gone. I glance down at the street. The lift operator has driven off.

"Fine by me," I say.

Martin gets up from the sofa, clambers up onto the windowsill, undoes the latches, and pushes the window wide open.

"You're sure about this?" he asks.

"Yes," I say.

He sticks one leg out into the air and balances on the other.

"Sure?"

"Yes!" I say.

So he gathers himself, bends his knees, hunches his back, stretches out his arms as if they were wings, and for a moment there I find myself thinking, He's going to jump, he's going to jump out of my window, a strange man is going to jump out of my window and smash himself to pieces, and how am I going to explain this to everyone, and I scream.

"No!" I scream. "For Christ's sake, don't!"

And I grab hold of him, and he laughs and jumps down to the floor and says, One–nothing, and I say, Go to hell, and he says, But you told me to do it, and I say, Get out, crazy strange man, out of my door, down the stairs, okay? and he kisses my cheek and strokes my hair and says, I'm not leaving, you know that, and I say, Yes you are. But by this time we both know he won't be leaving.

I HAVE A PATIENT, a woman in her thirties with cancer. She hasn't long to live. She tells me she has begun to think of herself in the third person. She is more than one self, she says. She is more than just the here-and-now and a body that has broken down, more than this one breast that only serves as a reminder of the other breast, more than a voice that says *I'm afraid, I'm afraid I can't stand this anymore.*

And then she says, "I breathe and it hurts. I breathe and it hurts. I breathe and it hurts."

I moisten her tongue.

"But sometimes," she says, "it seems like I get up, walk over to the window, and turn around to look at the woman in the bed. I hear her breathe in, and it doesn't hurt; I hear her breathe out, and it doesn't hurt. She breathes in, breathes out. She is not hurting. She is not hurting anymore. She is somewhere else now."

Stella Descending

HIS FINGERS FINDING their way into my panties, his hands parting my thighs, his cock driving into me, up inside me, I can't wait, his teeth around one nipple. My pussy bleeding, my breast bleeding. I beg him, Don't make me wait any longer. Sometimes, when Martin and I fuck, I lose my mind. I disappear, I'm done away with, I no longer exist. Split asunder. I am his breath, his fluids, his member, his blood.

MAYBE A MONTH before Martin rides up to my window on a sofa and installs both it and himself in my apartment, I have a visit from a plumber.

The pipes in the bathroom have started to act up: One day I get only cold water from the faucet, the next only hot. The bathroom is old and dingy, altogether pretty gross, but it has a nice big bathtub. I speak to the landlady, a tightfisted little woman in her sixties, crabby and pigheaded, and naturally she has no intention of helping me.

"What do you expect?" she says. "You're bound to have problems like that, with the rent as low as it is. You're lucky to be living here at all, when there's plenty of folks more in need of an apartment like yours."

This is how I come to look in the Yellow Pages under PLUMBERS and call a company that has only taken out a small ad. I have the idea that companies with small ads are cheaper.

I explain my problem to the woman who answers the telephone: the office secretary, I presume. I tell her that one day I'm getting only cold water, and the next I'm getting only hot. She says she'll arrange for a plumber to come out the following day at ten o'clock. At ten o'clock the next morning, the doorbell rings. At the door is this huge guy in his late twenties who tells me he's the plumber and he's been asked to check out my mixer tap. I show him to the bathroom and explain that one day I'm getting only cold water from the faucet, and the next I'm getting only hot. He lies down on the floor and proceeds to grope around under the bathtub, making strange grunting sounds as he does so. I leave him there and settle myself in the living room, on the floor; I have no furniture yet, only a mattress in the bedroom and a desk in the guest room. I sit on the floor listening to the sounds the plumber is making under my bathtub. Grunting sounds. Running water. More grunting. I sit there on the floor for a long while. Occasionally I run an eye around the room and think that it wouldn't be a bad idea to get myself a sofa. It's at this point that I have the idea of a green sofa set in the middle of the room, a sofa green as an avocado. I sit on the floor a while longer. Eventually I become aware of silence in the apartment, something with which I am familiar, so I get up and go to the bathroom. The plumber is leaning against the wall, smoking a cigarette.

"Have you fixed it?" I ask.

"No," he says. "I'll have to come back tomorrow."

The next day he arrives early in the morning, eight o'clock, as arranged. I have to be at work by nine.

"Just shut the door behind you when you leave," I say.

"Okay," he says.

And then he asks when I'll be home.

I turn and look at him and hesitate for a moment before replying that I'll be on duty until four. "Ah-ha," he says. "All right then, okay, fine." And he lies down on the floor and gets to work.

It's closer to five when I get home, and he's still there in my apartment. He's standing against the wall, smoking a cigarette.

"Are you still here?" I say.

"Yeah," says the plumber. "But I'm just leaving. I'll come back tomorrow."

"Is that really necessary? I mean . . . it can't be that big a job, surely, and it's going to cost a fortune, you coming back here day after day."

"Yeah," says the plumber.

He looks at me. He is extremely tall, so tall that every time he looks at me he is also looking down on me—something I'm not used to, since I'm also kind of tall.

"I've fixed things, more or less," he says. "Instead of having cold water today, as you normally would, you'll get hot water, and instead of having hot water tomorrow, again as you should have, you'll get cold water."

He takes a puff of his cigarette.

"But that doesn't really solve your problem."

"No," I say, "it doesn't."

"So I'll be back tomorrow. But I can't get here before ten. Since you've got to get to work, maybe you should let me have a set of spare keys so I can let myself in."

"Oh, no. You must be joking," I say, with a little laugh.

He eyes me curiously.

"No," I say again. "I can't just give you the keys to my apartment."

He shrugs and starts to pack away his plumbing tools.

"Well, of course," I falter, "of course if you feel you need an extra day, and that all this can be fixed?" I wave my arms in the direction of the bathtub and the shower.

He shrugs again. Says nothing. I fumble in my pockets, find my key ring, unhook two keys, the spare for the main door downstairs and the spare for the door upstairs, and hand them over. He takes the keys, slips them onto his own loaded key ring, and goes on packing his things. Still he says nothing.

"So you'll be here tomorrow at ten, then?" I say, worried that I've offended him.

"Yeah, yeah," he mutters. He slings his bag over his shoulder and walks through the living room and out the door.

.   .   .

I'm late getting home from the hospital the next evening. It must be around eight. The TV is on in the living room, and the plumber is in the bathtub. The place is awash with water and foam. For some time I just stand in the doorway staring at him. It takes a while for him to notice me.

"There you are," he says, splashing his face with water and wiping it with the back of his hand.

"And there you are," I retort, pointing.

He nods. "That's that problem solved!" he says.

"So I see," I say.

"Look!" he says, turning on one faucet and then the other. Water gushes out into a bathtub that is already brimful. There are suds in his hair. He splashes noisily. "Hot water, yeah! Cold water, yeah!"

"I'm glad that's sorted out," I say. "How much is it going to cost me?"

"Well, there's sorted and sorted," he says. "This was only the start of your problems. The pipes under the kitchen sink are rusty. They could snap at any minute and spring a leak, and that's going to mean a lot of water damage both here and in the apartment downstairs—"

"That's not my problem," I break in. "I only rent the place."

"That's exactly what I thought," the plumber says, getting out of the bath. When he stands up I am struck once again by how big he is. I try to keep my eyes fixed on anything other than his body, not his eyes, not his chest, not his arms, not his stomach, not his cock, not his thighs. I stare at his toes, stare doggedly at his big toe, which is bronzed and rather hairy, with a freshly clipped nail.

"So I had a word with the landlady," he goes on. "Funny woman, by the way—and she said this was your responsibility, because your rent is so low, but that she was prepared to chip in,

if it really was that bad, so I said"—the plumber points to himself—"yes, it really was that bad."

He grabs a towel and wraps it around his waist. Then he
goes into my bedroom, leaving huge wet footprints on the
wooden floor, to fetch his jeans and T-shirt. The T-shirt is neon
red with TREAT YOURSELF TO A PLUMBER printed in big letters
across the front.

One night a few months later, Martin and I are lying in bed, talking. The plumber is in the room next door. He has moved in,
although I can't quite explain how that came about.

"Can't you tell him?" I whisper, turning to Martin in bed.
"Tell him he has to move out, move out right now, find a place of
his own. I can't bring myself to do it. And you're living here too,
now. We don't really need the little he pays us in rent."

I count on my fingers.

"His plumbing bills are actually bigger than what he pays in
rent," I say.

Martin looks at me. Our eyes have grown accustomed to the
darkness of the room. He squeezes my hand and says, sure, he
can talk to the plumber, that's not a problem, but he doesn't
think there's any hurry. He doesn't see the point in throwing the
man out on his ear at a moment's notice.

"Yes, tomorrow, at a moment's notice," I whisper. "Tomorrow morning early! Or what about now?"

"No, Stella." Martin is now whispering too. "I don't want to
fall out with the guy. I like him. He's not in *my* way. This is *your*
problem." Martin lets go of me. I feel like crying, but I seldom
cry for Martin to see.

We had a fight once. I can't remember what it was about. I
only remember that it was the first fight we'd had and that I
started to cry. He looked at me long and hard. Then he shouted
"One–nothing!" at me and walked out the door.

WHEN I WAS YOUNG, before we moved to the house with the big square windows, we lived for a while in the Sankthanshaugen district of Oslo. I had a friend there; Victoria Larsen was her name. Her father had been in Dachau during the war—he'd been helping Jews escape to Sweden, I think, and for that he was sent away. In Dachau he wheeled corpses from the gas chambers to the ovens. When I visited Victoria's house, he would often be lying screaming in the bedroom.

"Don't pay attention," Victoria would whisper. "He's only dreaming."

One day we tiptoed into the bedroom, crept over to the bed, and stood by the headboard gazing expectantly at his face, each clutching a Popsicle, ready to view the next dream. But there was no dream that afternoon, and we had to tiptoe out again when the Popsicles began to melt.

I remember wondering whether my hair might catch fire or something if he screamed and I was standing so close.

I haven't thought of Victoria Larsen's father for years. He must be long dead; I really don't know. And that's not the kind of story you want to hear, is it? You don't want to hear about war heroes who lie screaming in the night, do you? You're not exactly a hero, are you, Axel?

I can just see you tiptoeing through the war years, a man of shadows: gutless, jumpy, and faithless, but always with some cheap magic trick up your sleeve.

MARTIN ASKS ME if I will go to Høylandet with him for his
grandmother's seventy-fifth birthday party. I'm afraid of flying,
but he says it'll be fine. His grandmother's name is Harriet, and
that's what everybody calls her. It's quite a gathering: relatives,
neighbors, friends, and a funny old man they call Thorleif—her
lover, I think. Harriet, old and sprightly, sits enthroned at the
head of the table. There's ostrich and *kransekake* on the menu.
When Martin introduces me, I am eyed up and down in a way
I'm not sure I like. Harriet informs me that she is half blind: She
can see me perfectly with one eye and not at all with the other.
She says it's an advantage, seeing people like that. The one eye
can tell the other eye things that a pair of normal eyes would
never notice. She has the loveliest gray hair, gathered into a long
braid that hangs down her back. Her mouth is thin and tight, an
ugly mouth. I catch myself studying her mouth during dinner,
trying to figure out who I know with that same thin tight
mouth. To my horror I realize that the mouth it reminds me of is
Martin's. I look away.

There are a lot of children at the dinner table, children of all
ages, several of them hovering around Harriet. My eye is caught,
in particular, by a boy of about six, delicate as a moth, with a

black forelock that keeps falling in his eyes. There are so many new faces at this party that I find it impossible to keep track of who is related to whom, never mind remember all their names. In years to come, too, Martin's family will always seem like strangers to me. We will see them socially, invariably at large parties like this, but they always seem to be enough in themselves, with no time for me. When I eventually start taking Amanda to their parties, and even Bee, Martin's own daughter, I feel like an interloper. Or perhaps not even an interloper; it's as if I don't exist. To me they are like shadows on a wall, so maybe to them I too am a shadow. They have their rituals, organize their parties, tell their stories and their jokes, and it makes no difference to them whether I am there or not. Martin says I am imagining things, that they have welcomed me with open arms, showed me hospitality and warmth, and I'm the one with the problem, not them.

The thin boy with the black forelock trots at Harriet's heels when she leaves the table, tugs at her braid and at the skirt of her *bunad*, the folk costume favored for such occasions. She flicks him off like a fly, but he comes right back. I've been helping to clear the table and am on my way out to the kitchen with a pile of dirty dishes. I pull up short in the doorway and stand watching. Harriet is at the kitchen counter decorating a jelly mold (when are we supposed to eat that? I wonder, stuffed as I am with ostrich and cake). The boy is standing behind her, whispering, "Hey, hey, hey." He tugs at her skirt. "Harriet," he says. "Harriet!"

For a long time she ignores him, goes on decorating the jelly; then all at once she whirls around and slaps the boy's face so hard he falls to the floor. "For heaven's sake!" I say, and run over to the boy. The woman with the one blind eye and the one seeing eye turns back to her jelly mold.

"You hit him," I hiss. "You hit this child!"

The boy gets to his feet, puts a hand to his forelock, and

brushes it back. "Uh-uh," he says, looking at me. "Uh-uh," he repeats, and hightails it, slender as a strip of film, out the kitchen door.

I want to say, You can't go around hitting children like that, I don't care if it is your birthday or if you are an old lady, even if you are Martin's grandmother. But I don't say any of this. I say nothing. I stand stock-still, just staring—at her, at the linoleum floor on which the boy had sprawled only a moment before—and suddenly I'm not sure what I saw and what I didn't see.

"And who might you be?" she snaps.

I start. "I'm Stella," I say.

She turns to face the counter. "Ah, yes, that's right," she says to herself, "Martin's intended." And then she sort of sings out my name letter by letter—"s-t-e-l-l-a"—and hands me the jelly mold. "Would you mind taking this to the table, please?"

She glares at me with her good eye. The blind eye gazes into thin air—as if really it were listening to something.

I know she's said to have been the loveliest lass in all Høylandet, but I never could see it.

Later that night, on the way home from the party, we spot a flock of screeching ostriches galloping across the frozen lake. They've escaped from the farm, and we have to call for help.

Martin puts his arms around me and says that if I were to get pregnant tonight, and if the baby is a girl, we should call her Bea, after his Swedish great-grandmother, Beatrice. I don't say anything about the boy with the black forelock who was knocked to the floor. I don't mention that until years later.

Then: *"Harriet?"* he says, thunderstruck. "Harriet hit a child? You're crazy! You must've been imagining things, Stella!"

WHEN I AM DEAD, Martin will cut out my heart and put it on a scale. In the other pan of the scale he will lay an ostrich feather. If my heart is lighter than the feather, I will live forever. If my heart is heavier, it will be devoured by Ammut the beast, part crocodile, part lion, and part hippopotamus.

MY HOME IS WITH MARTIN. I believe you would like me to stay with you. You might even be a little bit in love with me. But we don't talk about such things. It would upset you if I were to hint at any such thing. For Christ's sake, Axel, you're forever dying. You know, sometimes you disgust me. I'm young, Axel! I'm not going to die. It's you who's going to die, not me. I tell you I want to have more children. This hurts you. Dirty old man. Splendid old man. Don't mind me. You know I love you.

There are a lot of things I don't tell you. For example, I don't tell you that Martin checks where I keep my contraceptive pills and makes sure I take them every night. He knows when I have my period and when it's time to start a new sheet. He's always the one who goes to the pharmacy to refill the prescription when I've run out.

He wouldn't hold Bee when she was born. He got out of it by saying he wasn't feeling well; it had nothing to do with Bee. He was also having nightmares and not sleeping well.

"Nightmares about what?" I asked.

To which he replied, "The hideous beast Ammut."

But it might not be the same with a new baby. Martin is changing as the years pass. He has always been good to me, in his way, and he seems to have taken to the girls now, too.

I think I am going to stop taking the pill, when the time is right.

Stella Descending

WE RENT a holiday cottage in Värmland, just over the border in Sweden: a wooden cabin painted red, surrounded by trees, and among the trees a lake where Martin and I swim naked at night.

Bee is four years old, Amanda is ten. They are good friends and don't fight the way most sisters do. In the morning Amanda takes Bee into the forest, where they will build tree houses, play with pinecones and insects, and tell fairy tales. Amanda has breasts now, a little bump on either side of her T-shirt. Her dark hair falls past her waist. She's starting to happen.

By the time my girls get back, Martin and I have set the table in the garden. Bee has brought presents from the forest—in my lap she lays a beetle, a tuft of moss, and a twig covered in green leaves.

Amanda wants to play Nintendo, but we don't have a TV out here in the country. She misses her best friend, Marianne. She misses the city. In the evening we take turns telling stories about ghosts and other creepy things. First me, then Amanda, then Bee, but Bee just shakes her head. She doesn't want to tell a story, she says, she only wants to know if I liked the beetle, the tuft of moss, and the twig covered in green leaves.

"Yes, yes, Bee," I say brusquely. "Of course I liked them."

. . .

Then comes the evening when it is Martin's turn to tell a story.

"Once upon a time there was a beast by the name of Ammut," he says. "It lived around these parts, deep in the forests of Värmland. This beast had an enormous appetite. It had to eat the heart of at least one child every week. And it had to be a heart that did not beat too hard (hearts that beat hard gave the beast stomachaches, hiccups, and other digestive problems), nor yet a heart that beat too slowly. It was his servant Poppel, a wicked sorcerer, who procured and prepared the children's hearts. He did this by casting an invisibility spell on the children. You see, the sorcerer knew that for every day a child is invisible, its heart will beat a little more slowly, and after three weeks it will be beating at just the rate the beast likes best of all: a little but not too much.

"The children's parents knew nothing about the beast in the forest, nothing about Poppel the wicked sorcerer. And one by one the children went missing. Their parents called and called for them, but in vain. Eventually the parents decided that their children must be dead, and they wept without stopping for seven days, maybe more.

"The children, who were not dead at all, just invisible, climbed up onto their parents' knees, clutched their parents' hands, patted their parents' cheeks, slipped into their parents' dreams at night. 'We're not dead,' they cried, 'we're alive!'

"But even though their parents heard their cries, they persisted in believing that the children were dead. They put the cries down to grief playing tricks on them, and after a while both the children's cries and the parents' grief subsided."

"Did their parents' grief really subside?" Amanda asks.

"Yes, after a while," Martin replies. "The invisible children put their heads together and came to the conclusion that the only way to win back their parents' love was to become visible again, and the only way they could become visible again was by venturing into the forest and finding the wicked sorcerer. No sooner said than done: One by one the children tramped off into the tall trees of the forest; one by one they were caught in a sack by the wicked sorcerer, who had known all along in the depths of his dark heart that the children would come in the end, because no one wants to be invisible for too long a time; and one by one they were boiled alive in a cauldron—"

"And then what?" Bee asks, breaking in.

"Then all Poppel the wicked sorcerer had to do was to cut out the children's hearts, which by now were beating neither too hard nor too slowly but at just the right rate, and serve them to the beast," says Martin. "Snip, snap, snout."

Amanda looks at Martin. It is not a pleasant look. "The children's hearts wouldn't be beating at all, would they, if the children had been boiled alive in a cauldron?"

"'S'right," whispers Bee, edging onto Amanda's lap.

"Poppel's a sorcerer," retorts Martin defiantly. "And sorcerers can do whatever they damn well please."

The next day, and this is what I wanted to tell you, Martin takes Bee into the forest. His story has scared her. I say, "Come on, take her for a walk in the forest and show her that there is no sorcerer and no beast."

I stand at the window, watching them walk along the path leading into the forest. She looks so frail under all that long black hair, and he looks so big. They walk along side by side. I think, Surely he could at least take her hand. *Come on, Martin, take her hand! Why don't you take her hand?*

I say nothing.

Amanda comes to stand beside me. She looks out the window. "He's going to walk off and leave her out there, isn't he?"

"No, Amanda," I say. "He's not going to walk off and leave her."

We stand at the window a little while longer.

"Look," I say, and I point, too eagerly, too brightly. "He's taking her hand! He's taking her hand, Amanda."

And they disappear among the trees.

AMANDA MINE-ALONE. That's what I call her sometimes. She has no father to speak of. I know you two spend a lot of time together, Axel, and that's fine, even though I wish she got on better with young people. The old geezer, that's what she calls you. Her best friend, Marianne, doesn't call very often these days, and as far as I know she has no other friends her own age. When she's at home she lies in front of the TV, playing Nintendo; she has this game she plays, with a princess who has to round world after world, falling from one level to the next and fighting the most terrible battles in her quest to find the key to the palace of the king.

Sometimes I can spend a whole night sitting on the edge of her bed. She sleeps on her tummy, the way she did as a baby. She's all grown up now, tall and—I was about to say beautiful, but beautiful isn't the right word, although men do follow her with their eyes when she walks down the street. She's curvy, with the sort of figure I never had. I can't see it on her, can't see it in her face, her sleep is deep and seems so peaceful, but I know she has horrific dreams, of mutilation and ghosts and murder. I wish I could take her in my arms and hug the nightmares out of her.

Can you hear me, Amanda? I wish I could be with you when it gets you this way.

. . .

When Bee was younger she loved her pacifier. She hung on to that pacifier as if it were her only link with the world. Without it, nothing: no night, no day, no mother, no father—no Bee, in fact. Amanda never used a pacifier, never sucked her thumb, never had a single cuddly toy or doll or tattered old blanket. But ever since she was a baby she has had the habit of rubbing her right index finger gently up and down the bridge of her nose, as if, in her sleep, she were inscribing these horrific dreams of hers on her face, scene by scene.

In the morning, at the breakfast table, she tells us what she has dreamed about, but at that time of day even the worst dreams seem to have their funny side. Bee thinks Amanda is telling stories and begs her to tell some more.

Amanda has a father. I don't even know for sure whether he's still alive. Probably is, and doing fine, but no help to anyone since he emigrated to Australia. He sent us a postcard once: *Dear Stella. Dear Amanda. I'm fine. Miss you. Stella—tell Amanda I love her! Hugs and kisses and all that.*

WE DON'T MAKE LOVE as often as we used to. We don't sleep, either. After Bee was born we used to lie awake night after night, on sheets drenched in sweat, following the sound of Bee's breathing in her bassinet. She never cried, but she kept us up all the same.

Sometimes, when we're not lying there looking at the black shawl that covers the window, I take Martin's hand and give it a squeeze. This used to be a sign. He knows what it means. But I'm not even wet when he climbs on top of me and butts his way inside. His orgasm is sudden and silent. Afterward, he goes downstairs to the kitchen, makes coffee, sits on the sofa, and gazes out at the blackness of the night, waiting for it to let up. I am full of his body fluids; they're running out of me. I'm alone in the room—apart from Bee, breathing in her bassinet. I stroke my breast, remember when I used to bleed with sheer pleasure. I soak my hands in his semen, rub my fingers up inside myself, back and forth, slowly, thinking of Martin not down there in the living room but here with me.

Here with me, until I can no longer hold back the tears.

BEE STARTS NURSERY SCHOOL when she is five. She doesn't say much, but she stares at all of us—the nursery-school staff, the children, Martin, me—with a look in her eyes that I cannot fathom. She has great big eyes, with room for plenty of grievance.

"We've hardly had time to make any mistakes," Martin whispers, "and yet the way she looks at me, anybody would think I'd robbed her of all joy or something."

Bee's hair is long and dark and beautiful, just like Amanda's. All the other girls at nursery school want to comb it, brush it, braid it. Bee lets them. Bee sits on a blue box and lets the other girls tie red ribbons in her hair. She has the patience of a saint. But when I ask her who has tied ribbons in her hair, she can't say for sure.

One morning I hear a cry from Bee's room. It comes from Martin. I'm in the kitchen making breakfast. It's Martin's turn to wake the kids. I hear a cry from the bedroom and race up the stairs. Bee is still asleep—his cry has not woken her—her dark hair spread across the white pillow.

"Lift her head," Martin hisses.

"What is it?"

"Aw, Jesus!" says Martin.

Stella Descending

I sit down on the edge of her bed, lay my cheek against Bee's, listen to her breathing. So faint, feeble almost. This is my child, I think; dear God, help us. I run my hand through her hair and whisper to her that it's time to wake up. A black bug crawls over my fingers. I run my hand through her hair again.

"Bee's got lice," I murmur. "It's quite common," I add, seeing the look of revulsion on Martin's face.

Bee wakes without a word, wraps her arms round my neck, lays her head against my chest. There are lice on the pillow and on the sheets, and when I brush her hair lice fall on the floor.

"There's no end to it," Martin says. "There's just no end to it."

I keep Bee home from nursery school and Amanda home from school. Amanda tells us a tale about a princess who is so beautiful that gold coins fall from her hair every time she combs it. In the evening she plaits her own hair together with Bee's. They sleep in the same bed. I find them like that, intertwined, two girls and one braid. My daughters.

I INHERIT SOME MONEY from Pappa, enough for Martin and me to take out a loan and buy a semidetached house with a garden on Hamborgveien, near the Lady Falls. I have the idea that everything will be different when we move. We'll be more like a normal family. I can just picture it: Martin, Amanda, and Bee, in the kitchen, in the garden, maybe even a dog. More life, I think. Yes, that's it. More life.

And at long last I have a good excuse to kick out the plumber. There is no way he is coming with us. I refuse to take the plumber with us to the new house.

"D'you hear me, Martin? I'm not taking the plumber!"

Martin looks at me. "But I've already told him he can rent the room in the attic. I thought that would be okay. We could do with the money. And you should never underestimate the value of having a plumber in the house."

"And what value would that be, exactly?" I ask.

"A plumber in the house, Stella! A plumber in the house! Does everything have to be spelled out?"

A few weeks after Bee's sixth birthday we move to our new home in Hamborgveien. Martin, Amanda, Bee, me—and the plumber in the attic.

I didn't think Pappa had any money. I thought he had a lot of debts, so the inheritance came as a surprise. The gift shop in Majorstua had to close when Miss Andersen, the sales clerk, died and the customers stopped coming. That was a long time ago. Pappa spent the last years of his life in a dark little cubbyhole of an office, strictly a one-man affair, in downtown Oslo. I never really took any interest in what he did there. To the extent that I thought about it at all, I imagined that he did nothing. It has always been tempting to resort to the word *nothing* when trying to describe Pappa. I can't help thinking of this song about a dead man, sitting in the corner of a diner, and nobody realizing he's actually dead as a doornail. The first time I heard it I thought of Pappa. I thought it was Pappa who was sitting in the corner of that diner, dead as a doornail, with nobody noticing.

I finally get around to going into his cubbyhole office to clear it out. Mamma can't be bothered, she says; it was a big enough job packing his clothes into cardboard boxes (two boxes) and delivering them to the Salvation Army. The rest is up to me.

I don't know whether she mourns for him. It's hard to tell. It was a perfectly ordinary Wednesday. They were sitting in the kitchen, Mamma and Pappa on either side of the kitchen table, under the blue ceiling light, eating dinner. Then Pappa died. He didn't topple over, he just sat there on his chair, almost as if it would have been bad manners not to, with the same straight back, the same pale blue eyes. There was nothing to indicate that a change, if one can call it that, had taken place. He simply stopped eating. His face might have turned a bit grayer when it happened, I don't know. In any case, Mamma didn't notice a thing until she began to clear the table and he still hadn't moved.

His office looks exactly as I expected: a brown desk, a brown chair, a brown bookcase. A computer. A grimy window overlooking a grimy backyard. White fluorescent tubes on the ceiling. I find invoices and catalogs, from which I gather that after the closure of the Majorstua store, Pappa had gone on selling bric-a-brac by mail order. Mail-order knickknacks: crystal swans, brass candlesticks, sherry glasses, china dogs, angels in every shape and form at prices to suit every pocket. I discover that he rents a small storeroom somewhere in Asker, to the west of the city. And as far as I can see, everything is in perfect order: no unpaid debts, no dissatisfied customers, no secret love affairs, no unknown son or daughter. Nothing.

It takes me some time to find the key to the desk's top drawer, which is locked. The key is tucked high up on a shelf out of sight, inside a ceramic pot that must once have held a plant. There's still some potting soil at the bottom. I dust off the key and unlock the drawer. Inside I find a photograph and an unfinished letter dated many, many years earlier. The photograph is of a fair and rather plump lady pushing fifty. She has full red lips. Although it's hard to say for sure, I would say she is a tall woman. I turn the photograph over. The name *Ella* is written on the back in green, my mother Edith's handwriting. And a year: *1979.*

I pick up the letter, immediately recognizing Pappa's neat, elegant hand:

Dear Ella,

I am writing to you yet again. Edith has told me you have decided to leave for good this time and she intends to go with you. My wife says she's going to leave me for you. I beg you, I beg both of you: Do not do this. Stella may be a big girl now, but she is still not grown up. Not quite fourteen. She needs her mother. You promised me you would wait until she was grown.

THEY ARE ALL DEAD NOW.

I sing to Bee. She lies in bed listening, silent and solemn-faced. She won't play with my hands the way Amanda did at that age.

"Night-night, Bee," I say, but I receive no reply. "Aren't you going to say night-night back, Bee?"

Bee turns to face the wall.

I sit there on the edge of the bed, staring at the back of that thin, clammy little neck. Then I get up and look in on Amanda.

"Hi," I say.

"Hi," she says.

"That's just about enough Nintendo for tonight," I say.

"Oh, but Mamma, there's this beast in the forest that I have to kill," she says, "and then the princess'll fall down into the next world."

I stretch out on the sofa and read. It is far too quiet in this new house of ours. Not a sound except the mechanical little melody churned out by Amanda's Nintendo game.

The silence has followed me all the way here.

I AM LYING on the sofa, reading, when Martin walks into the living room and says, "That's it, Stella, I'm leaving you. I've packed a bag. I've found myself a studio to rent. I can't take this any longer: the house, the kids, Bee . . . all of it. I can't take it."

"I don't believe you," I say. I don't look up but keep my eyes fixed on the page of my book. He's done this before.

He sinks down onto the sofa, lays his head on my shoulder, and bursts into tears.

"I can't stand it," he whispers. "I'm going to disappear if I stay here."

"I don't believe you're going to leave me," I say. "I don't believe you've packed your bag, and I don't believe you've found a place to rent."

Martin is still crying. I stroke his hair.

"It's all turned to ashes," he says.

"Yes, but I don't believe you're going to leave me," I say.

He lifts his head and looks at me. I can't make out whether it's a nice look or a nasty look. But I know he won't leave now. He'll stay with me a little longer.

The summer Bee turns seven I fall ill. It is the most glorious summer we've had in years. The sun shines every day, and it gets to the point where nobody feels uneasy about saying, I'm fed up with all this sunshine, it's about time we had some rain. Usually when people say they're fed up with sunshine, someone else says, Ssh, don't complain, the weather could break any time.

That's Martin for you. Martin always has to take me to task. "Be careful what you say!" he warns. "Watch your tongue! Hubris!"

Then one night I tell him I have a stomachache—it might even be something serious, I add.

"Knock on wood," says Martin.

We are sitting in the garden of our new house, drinking vodka. It's the middle of the night, about three o'clock, maybe half past, in the first pale light of dawn.

"Last time I was sick was when I had German measles as a kid," I say, laughing. "Just kidding. I'm never sick. Never!"

"This summer will never end, and you're never sick," Martin mutters.

"I've got a bit of a stomachache, that's all. Forget it,"

But the next morning the pain is worse. I have to stay in bed. When I throw up all over the eiderdown and the floor, I blame it on the vodka from the night before.

But it's got nothing to do with the vodka from the night before, it's something else, something growing inside me that's trying to do away with me, I think. Yes, that's it, something that's trying to do away with me. How come I didn't see it before? Late the next day Martin drives me to the hospital.

"I'm having contractions," I tell the doctor. By this time I'm in tears. "I'm having contractions, but I'm not pregnant. I'm dying. I'm going to die, aren't I?"

Then I lose the sound. I can see the doctor's lips moving, but I can't hear what he is saying. All I can hear is my own breathing, in, out, in, out, and I have a fleeting vision of the way in which, night after night, I still bend over Bee's bed when she's asleep to check that she is breathing, in, out, in, out, because Bee is the sort of child who could suddenly die on me. Bee is too good for this world. I turn to Martin to tell him this, that Bee is too good for this world—that this is something he has never understood, nor have I—but I can't get the words out. He wouldn't hear me anyway. He's too busy talking. Martin is talking and the doctor is talking, both looking at me, and Martin is fiddling with his car keys and I know that any second now he's going to drop his car keys, and I try to tell him that he's going to drop the car keys if he doesn't stop fiddling with them, but he wouldn't hear that either. And then he drops the car keys and there's a booming in my ears. He doesn't even notice. I bend down to pick them up, feel them in my hands, a familiar, coolish object between my fingers, such a prosaic thing, a bunch of car keys. I straighten up and try to say something to the doctor and Martin, because neither of them is moving his lips now. They are just staring at me. It's all I can do not to giggle, they look so solemn, they ought to be wearing black top hats and have black mustaches. Are you going to a funeral, I try to ask, it being such a lovely day and all? I put out my hand to show them I've picked up the car keys, smile my sweetest smile—then comes another boom and everything goes black.

Stella Descending

ONCE, A LONG TIME AGO, you told me you were now so old that you sometimes talked to—or at any rate sensed the presence of—the dead, that the boundaries between them and you were gradually fading. Dear Axel, I don't want to die yet. Pray for me. Ask them to stay away. I have two children. Give me a little more time.

I DO RECOVER EVENTUALLY, although the blood flows more slowly around my body and nothing has any scent anymore, not even the lilac in the garden. Sometimes I have the feeling that I am living on borrowed time.

I look at pictures of myself from just a few years back. Now I can see that I was almost beautiful. But today . . . I don't know.

I want him to fuck me until I wake up. I want him to fuck me back to the days when I used to bleed with joy.

I place the pill on the back of my tongue and swallow the water. As he turns away to set the glass down on the bedside table, I spit it out again and crush the pill between my fingers. I slide into bed, under the eiderdown, and take his cock in my mouth. This time he doesn't push me away. He's grown hard, he turns me onto my stomach, he presses my face into the pillow. I'm not breathing, oh, no, I'm not breathing. From behind he finds his own way into me and comes with a gasp.

BEE HAS HER EIGHTH BIRTHDAY. She says she would like a dog. Martin doesn't want a dog. I don't really want a dog either. But Bee wants a dog, and Amanda wants a dog.

"A dog wouldn't be that much trouble, surely," I say. "Not now that we've got a house."

Martin shrugs.

"Bee doesn't play with other children," I say. "Nobody ever comes home with her after school; she never gets invited anywhere. She's lonely."

"Aren't we all," says Martin. "Dog or no dog."

We find a dog through an ad in the newspaper. A family on Nesodden wants to find a home for their eight-month-old mongrel. We're away a lot, they say, we don't have the time, he's well-behaved, house-trained, affectionate. The dog is gray with white paws and a white tip on his tail, little and scrawny with a big dry nose. His name is Hoffa—after Jimmy Hoffa, the union leader. Not the most fitting name, Martin and I feel, for such a little scrap of a thing, an awful lot to live up to, but a name's a name. And Hoffa does everything Bee says. Bee says *Sit*, and Hoffa sits. Bee says *Down, boy*, and Hoffa lies down. Bee says *Come*, and Hoffa comes. Bee says *Give me a paw*, and Hoffa lays his paw in

Bee's hand. At night Hoffa sleeps under Bee's eiderdown, curled in against her stomach. During the day he sits on the windowsill or in the garden, waiting for her to come home.

One day, Hoffa wriggles through a hole in the fence out into the street. He sits himself down on the sidewalk and takes a sniff at two girls walking past. The girls are not strangers, they are neighbors' kids, in the same class as Bee. At one point the plan had been for these girls and Bee to walk to and from school together, but nothing ever came of it. The girls didn't want to; it was as simple as that. Their parents apologized for the fact that the arrangement had not worked out as expected. That was a long time ago.

But now Hoffa is sitting on the sidewalk in front of our house. He sniffs at the girls walking past, and maybe he rubs up against them the way he usually does when he wants to be scratched behind the ears. But the girls have no intention of scratching behind his ears. They lift their sneaker-clad feet and kick Hoffa in the side, so hard he falls over.

I see none of this. Bee is the sole witness. She is a little farther up the road when it happens.

"No!" she shouts, and races toward the girls. "Don't kick him!" she shouts. "Don't kick him! Please!"

The girls turn to look at her. They snigger.

"Stupid old dog!" they yell. "Stupid old dog!"

Hoffa whimpers, still lying on the sidewalk. Flat out, as if trying to hide his skinny doggy body in the pavement, as if hoping the ground will open up and swallow him. Nose between his paws.

The girls kick Hoffa again, hard, in the stomach this time; then they both run off.

Bee stops short, turns her face to the sky, and screams. If you didn't hear her, only saw her, as I suddenly catch sight of her through the living room window, you would have thought she was standing there on the sidewalk with her face turned to the sky, singing. But then I hear her. I hear that she is screaming—and then, only then, do I run out to ask my little girl what has happened.

Sometimes I have the thought—no, I never voice it, but I do think it—that Bee is not mine, even though, at great discomfort to both herself and to me, she fought her way out of my body, in no uncertain terms, over eight years ago. Sometimes I have thoughts I don't want to have, pictures that come unbidden. *A cuckoo in the nest! Bee is not one of us! Bee is an interloper!* I look at her, this strange, awkward, quiet little girl whose hand always shakes slightly, and feel nothing but exasperation, even anger, that she should be there at all, in my sight. Is it okay for me to think like that? No! No! It's not that simple. Because at the very moment that this thought strikes me, all I want to do is to draw her close and assure her of how much I love her.

Could it be that wanting to love someone so much is also love of a sort?

Our neighbors, the girls' parents, do eventually apologize for the incident with Hoffa, but not without observing that the dog was running loose in the street and that the girls were afraid and acted in self-defense.

Me, I sit night after night by Bee's bed. She has pulled the eiderdown right over her head, like a little animal gone into hibernation. I try to push the quilt aside so I can stroke her cheek, but she screams *no!* or something like that, and pulls the eiderdown back over her head.

IS IT RIGHT that the dog's nose is warm and dry?

Is it right that Bee never cries?

Is it right that the lilac in the garden has no scent?

Is it right that Amanda has to fall from world to world?

Is it right that this house is so quiet?

Is it right to have a plumber living in the attic, sending us plumbing bills we cannot pay?

Is it right to have a mother who would rather be a tree?

Is it right that I come to see you and stand in front of the gilt mirror in your hallway and see your face instead of my own?

Is it right that Martin and I never sleep?

Is it right that in the forest there lives a beast who eats children's hearts?

Over the window in our bedroom we have hung a black shawl to block out the light. In some places the shawl is worn thin, in others it is still thick. Because of these irregularities in the fabric, not all the light is kept out, and it forms patterns and pictures on the black screen that we can look at when we lie in bed.

Now and then a face seems to present itself on the shawl. Martin sees a woman's face. I see a man.

We call the face Herr Poppel.

Long ago, when I was pregnant with Bee, we called her Herr Poppel. Before that we called the plumber Herr Poppel. In my mind I have called you, Axel, Herr Poppel. I think almost anyone can be Herr Poppel, good or evil, big or small, dead or alive.

JUST BEFORE SHE DIES Mamma comes to me. She is a patient in my ward, though she does not want me to nurse her. She is ashamed of her illness, of her body. Nonetheless, I insist on nursing her. I don't quite know why, what my motives are. We don't say much to each other. I tend to her, wash her, feed her, and fluff her pillows, all with the hands of a professional. Mamma says, I have a daughter and my daughter has hands; and I say, You have a daughter and she is a nurse and she tends to you just as she tends to all the others—there's no more to it than that. But one morning I stand by her bedside and watch her while she is sleeping. The disease has disfigured her, but at this particular moment her face is as beautiful as it used to be. Maybe it's the morphine. Or maybe it is death, putting a period at the end of the sentence, death saying, *This is your mother's face as it was when it was loveliest. Forgive her or strike her. But leave it at that.*

I sit down on the edge of the bed, still gazing at her, and she senses that I am close by, that I want something of her. Even with her body pumped full of morphine she senses it. Just as she opens her eyes, I lean over her and hiss, "Tell me about Ella!"

"No," she says.

"Yes," I say.

I rummage in my pockets and produce a tattered photograph of a plump woman with full red lips.

"I found this picture in Pappa's desk drawer," I say. "How many years had he been holding on to this picture, do you think? Fifteen? Twenty? How many times a day did he take it out of that drawer and look at it?"

Mamma raises her hands, wasted old hands that betray her face, hands that say the beautiful face on the pillow is nothing but a mirage. She snatches the picture and grips it tightly between her index and middle fingers. I could easily snatch it back, but I don't. I let her keep it. She doesn't look at it: doesn't need to or doesn't want to.

"We were painfully attached to one another. That's all there is to it, Stella. I would have followed her to the ends of the earth if she had asked me to."

Mamma breathes out, breathes in, breathes out, breathes in.

"Does it hurt?" I ask.

"No," she says.

"Yes it does," I say.

"No," she says.

Her stomach rumbles. We both start. I am sitting on the edge of the bed, holding her hand. She tries to pull away, but I keep a firm grip. I've never heard Mamma's stomach rumble. She cringes, looking as if she would like to hide under the covers. Her eyes plead with me: Leave me alone, go away. But I stay where I am.

"You're not going to die alone," I say.

"But that's what I want," she whispers.

"Maybe so," I say, giving her hand a squeeze. "But you're not going to die alone."

And then she farts. Mamma lets off a rotten, rasping, spluttering fart that must have been stewing away inside her ever since the time when she decided, as a little girl, to become as quiet as a tree. Mamma farts, opens her eyes wide, and says, "Go away, go away," and then she shuts her eyes, breathes in, breathes out, and dies.

I lean over her, put my lips to her ear. "Now you're a tree," I whisper.

Afterward I take off my shoes. I lie down beside her on the bed. I am going to lie here for a while. Later on I'll iron the white blouse, wash the old body, and comb the lovely long hair that I longed to play with when I was a little girl, even though she never liked it when I touched her.

IT IS NIGHTTIME. The bathroom is lined with mirrors so I can see that my face is pale and blotchy. I unpack the pregnancy test kit, hold the stick between my legs, and pee over both the stick and my hand. I remain seated on the toilet, waiting for the result. Slowly the blue line starts to show. A blue sky, I think to myself. A blue dress. A blue sheet. I get up from the toilet seat, stand in front of the mirror, and breathe out, making my stomach swell. It will be some months before it really starts to show. A blue vein over my hip bone. When I breathe in I can see my ribs. Mamma once told me I was so skinny that I looked like something out of Belsen. I didn't know what Belsen was, but I thought it was great to have Mamma make any comment at all about my body. There is a fetus growing inside me. I can picture those photographs by Lennart Nilsson. A blue fetus. Blue water. Blue hands. Slowly I am going to be brought back to life. Slowly I am going to be brought back to life, and Martin will be able to sleep again, with no dreams.

In a minute I'll go down to Martin and say, Listen to me! Put down that video camera. I haven't been swallowing the birth control pills you've been giving me, not for ages. I want to hear a baby crying in this house. I don't want all this silence.

I THINK OF YOU, Axel. You are so old. It is not your face I see now. It is not your face I see in the mirror. It is mine. I am Stella. I am thirty-five years old. I live here, in this house. It is August 27, 2000. Soon it will be morning. Next spring I am going to have a baby, and by that time you are sure to be dead. Which is as it should be.

(IV)

FALL

I was standing there, scissors in hand, snipping away, when I saw it.

Some girls had come running over to me with a long piece of rope they had found behind a tree in the park. They wanted to know if I had a pair of scissors and would cut the rope in half, to shorten it. They wanted to use it for a jump rope, they said.

Why, of course I have scissors, I said, opening my purse. I always carry a pair of scissors.

The girls weren't really paying any attention to me. They stood in a huddle, sharing a bag of candy, talking among themselves and waiting for me to do as they asked. They cannot possibly have seen what I saw.

What did I see?

I saw a man and a woman, way over there, way up there on the roof, and both of them dangerously close to the edge. They teetered back and forth, back and forth, and I wanted to shout at them to stop it, to get down from there; they were putting their lives at risk. But I was far too far away. I was in the park; they were up on the roof. We were separated not only by a street but by cars and people and trees. And then she tripped toward him. The woman tripped into the man and he caught her in his arms, and they stood there embracing for ages. I breathed out, relieved, turned to the girls, cut the rope—and saw her fall.

I saw her fall. A flutter, a movement in the corner of my eye. The rest of my gaze was on the girls, the park, the trees—all that greenery. I saw her fall, a dark speck on the edge of a green picture.

But if you ask me whether she tripped, was pushed, or jumped, I could not say. Nor is it any of my concern.

Axel

As to Stella's funeral, there's not much to say. She's ashes now.

The walk in the sunshine from Majorstuen to the crematorium was not pleasant, partly because I got sunburned, on the back of my neck and my earlobes—it still hurts, and putting cream on the afflicted areas does no good—and partly because the blister on my right foot made it virtually impossible for me to walk the whole way in my new shoes, with the result that I arrived at the chapel of the crematorium limping and close to tears. Usually when I go for a walk, I wear a pair of gleaming-white sneakers, but that would never have done for today. A black suit and gleaming white sneakers is not a happy combination, not unless you're a pop star or something of the sort. Naturally, I did consider walking to the chapel in my sneakers and changing into my dress shoes for the funeral, but I have never approved of carrying one's good shoes to one's destination in a plastic bag, as my fellow countrymen are given to doing—when it snows, for example. And I could just imagine what insurmountable difficulties this alternative would present in terms of the actual changing of the shoes. First I would have to find a bench close to the chapel—a little out of the way so as not to attract any attention—then untie the laces, remove the sneakers, and put on my dress shoes. Then I would have to put the sneakers in the bag and, in short, show myself to be, or have become, the very sort of man I despise: a man who carries his shoes in a plastic bag. So there you have it, the reason I did not opt for this alternative and the explanation for my hobbling into the chapel, tortured and tearful. You know, it is remarkable how a measly blister can completely overshadow such entities as God and death. As the service got under way, I could not have cared less what the minister had to say about anything whatsoever. I had only one thing on my mind: whether it would be possible to unlace my right shoe and kick it off—during the first hymn, perhaps—without the other mourners noticing, and by doing so ease my right foot. This I succeeded in doing, and the minute the shoe was no longer pressing on the blister, the pain stopped. What bliss! Such was the relief that although I did not mean to, I simply could not help but utter a loud *ahhhh!*

At that, an elderly woman with eyes as big as saucers turned to look at me and held my gaze. Everyone was singing, but this woman had heard me. I knew because the look she gave me was a stern one, and this so unsettled me that I let out another *ahhhh!*, this time putting into my voice all the anguish I could muster, in order to persuade her that what she was hearing were the sounds of an old man sobbing over the death of a young woman and not the blissful sighs of an old man easing his aching foot. The strange woman's eyes promptly softened, and she even smiled a sympathetic smile. Then she nodded, and I nodded, confidentially, sorrowfully, eloquently, as people are wont to nod to one another at times of mourning.

I was sitting well to the back of the chapel. I did not speak to anyone except Amanda, little dark-haired Amanda, with fury in her blue eyes and one arm wrapped protectively around her sister, the quiet one. There weren't many people there. Martin, of course, and three old women, each uglier than the one before, the least hideous being the lady with whom I had exchanged such eloquent nods. There were other people there, too, but, as I say, not many. The chapel was empty and silent. I thought it odd that not more people had shown up. But perhaps another ceremony was being conducted elsewhere. Perhaps Stella's friends and workmates were actually somewhere else, in a church maybe, not here with us. I ran an eye over those in attendance: pale unapproachable strangers, not here with us, the dying. In my mind's eye I saw people bursting with life, a packed flower-bedecked church, eulogies, comforting hands.

I have tried, over the years, to imagine Stella's day-to-day life. Did she laugh and cry with girlfriends, attend dinner parties, cast her vote at election time, talk on the telephone, read the newspaper, dance until the wee small hours, write letters, go skiing (no, now that I come to think of it, she never went skiing; that I do know), frequent cafés, take part in demonstrations, campaign for—yes, for what?—read books, see films, listen to music? Oh, dear little Stella. My dear Stella.

Once the coffin had been duly lowered into the floor, I slipped my right foot into my shoe, tied the laces, and walked out, more or less erect, into the late-August light. I offered my condolences to Martin, that pompous ass, who did not deserve her. He thanked me and looked away. Finally, I limped off in the sunlight to pick up my old blue Volkswagen Beetle from the repair shop.

That was when it happened. Just as I was getting into the car to drive off after a lot of hemming and hawing, Amanda suddenly whipped open the door on the other side, jumped into the front seat, and said, "Come on, drive! Let's get out of here!" Her mischievous blue eyes were full of tears, her hair messed up, her cheeks blotched. Over her plum-colored dress she was wearing a long baggy black cardigan.

"But Amanda, dear," I whispered, "why aren't you with your family?"

"Drive, Axel!" she screamed.

I started the car and turned out onto the road. The miles

don't exactly fly by when I'm behind the wheel. Amanda sighed under her breath, obviously wishing I would step on it. With what in mind had the child followed me from the crematorium to the repair shop and jumped into the car? That we would drive off a cliff and into the sunset, like a couple of outlaws from the Old West? It was on the tip of my tongue to tell her that if you're going to turn your life into a drama, you need to choose your co-stars with care. An old man with a Volkswagen Beetle was not what she needed right now. Had I been seventy years younger, maybe, and driving an old Ford—but I bit it back. I felt deeply sorry for her, but there was nothing I could do other than drive her to the house on Hamborgveien where she lived. And I was tired. I wanted to go home. I wanted to be alone.

"I don't have a family," Amanda said.

"Excuse me?"

"You asked why I wasn't with my family, and I said, *I don't have a family*."

"You have a sister who needs you," I said. "You have to be brave now, for Bee's sake."

It occurred to me that I was being rather harsh, telling a fifteen-year-old who had just lost her mother that she had to be strong for someone else, even if the other person was younger and weaker than herself. After all, it was true what she said: Amanda had no family, apart from Bee. As far as I knew, Amanda's father was in Australia—if he was still alive, that is. Stella never talked about him.

"Bee's too good for this world," muttered Amanda. "That's what Mamma said. And now she's got nobody but the ostrich king—"

"And you, Amanda," I interrupted.

"I don't know about that," she mumbled. "Don't know about that."

We drove for a while in silence. At Ullevål Hospital I turned into Sognsveien.

"Are you taking me home now, Axel?" she asked.

"Yes."

"Couldn't I come to your place for a while instead? Please? Couldn't we play cards, or drink cocoa, or do magic, or just have a bit of a chat . . . about Mamma or whatever? I don't want to go home!" Her voice was close to breaking. "I don't want to go home!"

A little girl, a little dark-haired girl, sits in my car, crying and saying she doesn't want to go home, and there is nothing I can do. I cannot, I don't know how.

"Not now, Amanda," I said wearily. "I'm taking you home."

"Please. I—"

"Not now!"

She's not mine, I thought to myself. She is not mine.

Stella was mine . . . my friend. Amanda is not mine.

I drove, and the girl wept, and all I wanted was to get out of this.

"I think he pushed her," she said, out of nowhere. "The police were at the house all night, talking to him. Martin's a murderer, just so you know."

"No, he's not, Amanda," I replied despairingly. "You're letting your imagination run away with you. In cases like this the police always interview the immediate family. It's . . . routine."

She turned and looked at me. Even from where I sat behind the wheel, I could see the look in her eyes, the fury.

"Why couldn't you have died instead?" she blurted out. "You're old, you've been around for almost a hundred years, you've got no children who care about you, you're tired, worn out, decrepit, you've got no guts, and you probably can't wait to die."

"You're right about that, Amanda," I replied softly, turning into Hamborgveien. "And if it were up to me I'd be only too happy to take Stella's place."

I brought the car to a halt outside the house. A garden with a scattering of withering flowers in a bed next to the fence, a lawn that needed cutting, and a flag at half mast. No lights in the windows. There were no plans for any sort of reception after the funeral. Martin's car was parked on the street outside, so I took it that he was home.

"Is it all right if we say goodbye here, Amanda?"

I had no wish to see her to the door and have to stand there talking to the widower.

Amanda made no move to get out.

I opened the door on my side and squirmed my way out, bumping my head on the rim; I was aching all over—my head, my back, my hip, my right foot. Okay, I thought, now this young lady is getting out whether she likes it or not. I limped around to the other side, opened the door, and said, "Amanda! You're going to get out of my car this minute, and then I'll get back in, shut the door, and drive home to my apartment. I am an old man!"

She buried her face in her hands and wept. "I'm so alone, Axel. I'm so awfully alone."

I cast a glance all around. Wasn't anyone going to come and help me out here, keep me from having to ring the doorbell and explain the situation to the man in there? No one came. But Amanda stopped crying, pulled her cardigan tight around herself, and got out of the car. She did not say a word, merely sniffed a little. Wiped her face with the back of her hand. She walked up to the house, without looking back.

"Goodbye, Amanda," I called.

No reply. I saw that slim back, a child's back, and the new angular hips that would soon be catching men's eyes, if they weren't already.

"This is a difficult time," I called. "Maybe you could come and see me in a day or so, and I'll teach you a new trick . . . or we can just talk, if you like."

She did not turn around. I saw her stop outside the main door, hunt for something in her cardigan pocket, produce a key, and let herself into the house.

.   .   .

Nothing today has gone as I planned. I did not, for instance, have time to buy my entrecôte of venison or my bottle of Châteauneuf-du-Pape, and there's nothing in the house to eat except half a loaf in the bread bin, a banana, and some instant coffee. Two hours until the evening news. Money Sørensen went home hours ago. She has cleaned and dusted, but in her usual slapdash fashion. There are fingerprints on the mirror in the hall. Next time she comes I'm going to tell her what I think of her. Not that she's an old hag, I won't say that. I will be extremely civil, but I will make it quite clear that I feel the time has come for us to go our separate ways.

I fetch a cloth and try to wipe off the fingerprints. For a moment I think I see Stella's face in the mirror.

"I miss you," I sniff. "I'm aching all over."

She looks puzzled.

I shut my eyes. She is still there. Her face, back there, in my mind's eye.

"I want to be with you," I whisper. "Come, let me be with you."

And now what? What about the remainder of this wretched day? First of all I am going to put on my gleaming-white sneakers and walk down to the newsstand manned by the girl with the blank eyes. I am going to say, "You don't know me, you don't remember my face, but every morning I buy the same five newspapers from you, as I did today before getting dressed to go to my friend's funeral. Right now, though, I don't want any newspapers. What I want is cigarettes. Give me a pack. Doesn't matter which brand. And to hell with everything and everybody."

Amanda

I've laid myself down on the bed beside Bee. Her red dress was itching, so I took off her funeral clothes and found her a pair of sweatpants and a T-shirt. Bee's room has never been fixed up. It's mostly white—white walls and a wooden floor painted white—not bright white but dingy. The ceiling is blue, but in a lot of places the blue paint has flaked off and underneath the blue it's red, and under the red it's yellow. I tell Bee that lots of people have lived in this old house, and in this very room, too. The first person to live here was a lady who painted the ceiling yellow to remind her of the sun.

"Why did she do that?" whispers Bee.

"Because this lady was never allowed to go outside and look at the real sun," I say. "She was held prisoner by a beast who was in love with her. But then the lady gave birth to a little boy, and he lived in this room with his mother, and together they painted the ceiling red to remind them of"—I had to think for a minute—"to remind them of sugar candy, because sugar candy was the boy's favorite thing of all."

"So did the beast let him have sugar candy?"

"No," I say. "Of course the beast didn't let the boy have sugar candy, but his mother had been given sugar candy when she was a little girl, and she told the boy all about it. Just listening to her made him long for sugar candy.

"They used to lie side by side in bed, like we're doing now, before they fell asleep, and while they were lying there she would tell him about the times she had sugar candy when she was a little girl."

"But who painted the ceiling blue?" asks Bee.

"That was the beast," I say. "One evening the mother wrapped her arms around her son, got out of bed, and jumped out of that window over there, and they fell and fell without ever hitting the ground. They rounded one world after another and never had to come back here. And the beast was so sad he painted the ceiling blue."

We are both stretched straight out on the bed. Bee runs her hands down the legs of her sweatpants. She's breathing softly and steadily, but her eyes are open, full of wonder. Maybe she'll fall asleep soon. I stroke her cheek gently. Her skin is dry. Mamma used to put cream on her face. Bee would sit perfectly still on the bed, gazing at Mamma. Sometimes she would fling her arms around Mamma's neck before Mamma had finished putting on the cream. This made Mamma cross. I could tell by the look on her face, but she would stay where she was until Bee let go of her. Bee gives long hard hugs. It's kind of difficult to break free.

Nobody knows Bee better than me, but there are lots of things I don't know about. There are lots of things I don't know about being in charge of children, I mean, because now I'm in charge, and we can't stay here with the ostrich king. No way. Lots of fifteen-year-olds have children. There's this girl at school who got pregnant. She had an abortion. I've even read about twelve-year-olds who've had babies. It happens all the time. Twelve-year-old girls give birth to their babies when they go to the bathroom. Suddenly there's a *plop* and there it is: a baby. I wonder what it's like to stare down into the toilet bowl into those eyes. I think I'd pull the plug fast, flush it away before either of us started crying.

Before, when I was younger, I used to think about things like that a lot. Especially that summer we spent in Värmland—Mamma, Martin, Bee, and me. There we had to use an outhouse. And when I sat there, particularly once darkness had fallen in the evenings, I used to bang my feet on the walls of the outhouse to scare away rats and any other nasty things crawling around down there. The beast has long skinny arms. I was sure that one day I would feel his hands on my behind, that he would curl his fingers round my hips and drag me down into the shit alongside him.

And now Mamma's been buried. Or, not exactly *buried*. The coffin disappeared into a hole in the floor, down and down until we couldn't see it anymore. I didn't know that was how they did it. There's this secret hatch that slides open and the coffin disappears. And the minister didn't so much as blink an eye, not once. It was a bit like the time the plumber and I managed to round the last world and finally found ourselves within striking distance of the king's palace. A hatch opened in the floor, and we were imprisoned in a castle, but then another hatch opened and we got free. But what about the coffin? Is there a floor underneath the chapel floor and another floor underneath that one? She won't give in, not Mamma. She's still falling. She goes on falling and falling even after she reaches the ground. Do you hear me, Bee? Mamma's still falling. She falls through layer upon layer of fire and earth and sand and roots. I don't think there's any bottom.

The plumber didn't come to the chapel. He said he would be there, but instead he packed his things and left. Pappa wasn't there either. To be honest, I'm glad he wasn't. I don't think Pappa and I would get on very well. I heard Mamma say once that Pappa went to Australia because he wanted to get as far away from her as possible—and Australia was the farthest-away place he could think of. I wasn't supposed to hear that. Mamma was talking to the old geezer. But the old geezer doesn't hear what people say, that's the trouble with him.

Mamma said a lot of things I wasn't supposed to hear. She would talk and talk: to Martin and to the old geezer. But I have two big ears. I don't miss much. And one day I'm going to tell Bee all the things I can't tell her right now.

Axel

When Dr. Isak Skald, my only true friend, insisted that I stop smoking, he did so on the grounds that if I did not it would kill me. This has never struck me as being a decent argument. Nevertheless, I did stop. When I attempted to start smoking again I was prevented from doing so by his widow, Else, that marvelous woman with the hands that could change a man's life. In any case, the joy was gone. I smoked cigarette after cigarette, but joylessly, so why bother? But if I had gone on smoking, and if Skald's medical observations were correct, as I have no doubt they were, I would probably be dead by now. I make myself a cup of instant coffee. Half an hour until the evening news. I, Axel Grutt, widely known as Gruesome Grutt the schoolteacher, am still alive. Why do my days on this earth never end? I am nothing but wasted flesh, and yet my heart is still beating. Is it really just going to go on like this?

> *Who leads me then to your refreshing rill?*
> *'Tis death so still.*

WHEN THIS DAY, Stella's day, is over, I shall light a candle, or two, or three.

First I will light a candle for my wife, Gerd. *Now listen to me, Axel, because this is going to hurt.* I can see her now. That yellow sweater. The defiant look in her eyes. The provocative air about her that I was to come across again, years later, in Stella. I have suffered physical afflictions for as long as I can recall. But afflictions of a physical nature were not what Gerd had in mind. That is not what she was talking about.

"So what was she talking about?"

"Oh, Stella, there you go again, always probing and prying!"

"Yeah, well, I'm curious."

"Is it the shame of it that hurts you?" Gerd asked, when I begged her to stay. She was sick and tired of the whole business. She had had enough. She wanted to get away. She was going to take little Alice and go north with this other man. Of course, I should have let her go. Instead I asked her to stay. Don't ask me why.

Victor was his name: her lover. A fellow teacher. Blond and handsome and very popular with the pupils. Gerd was besotted with him long before we were married, and he with her. Oh, dear me, yes. They were meant for each other right from the start. I was the big mistake, her life's tragedy, the tumor in her stomach. But it was Gerd's choice, and Gerd chose me. Because I could do magic. And he could not.

Once upon a time, a long time ago, Victor and I were good friends. It all started in the thirties, when we were students. I used to meet him at the Trocadero. I remember him well. On one occasion he kept an entire table entertained with love poems he had written himself, apparently inspired by Gerd Egede-Nissen the actress, whom, not surprisingly, he had never met. But there was another Gerd in Victor's life—and the poems were, of course, addressed to her. And she, Gerd number two, was sitting at our table that evening, looking every bit as lovely as Gerd number one.

She liked us both. Victor recited poems; I did conjuring tricks. In the beginning she could not choose between us. Then one evening I magicked away her wristwatch, the gold barrette from her hair, her hat, her scarf, and the crucifix she wore around her neck. I threatened to magic away her blouse, her stockings, and her skirt, too, if she would not marry me, so she said yes. I felt I had won fair and square, but Victor refused to admit defeat.

"It's me she wants," he said. "This way you're only going to ruin both your lives."

"But I'm a better magician than you are a poet," I said.

He looked at me long and hard. "And what about the wedding night?" he said. "And the night after the wedding night, and the night after that? Are you going to pull a rabbit out of a hat then too?"

That was when I told him to shut up.

Gerd and I were married in 1936. She endured it for a few months; then she went running back to him. He was waiting for her, welcomed her back with open arms, and I let them get on with it. I don't know what was worse, their infidelity or their contempt. Their contempt, I think. The fact that they were laughing at me, in a mildly pitying, resigned sort of way. That was the worst. I was not a bad man; I wasn't. I was a small man. I was a pathetic man. I was the kind of man other men would have spat on had they known. But I was not a bad man.

We had a deal, Gerd, Victor, and I; we made a pact: No one was to know. No one. This was to be our secret, our dirty little secret. This was between us three. Then came the war. Victor was one of the key figures on the coordinating committee of the teacher's union—later banned—to which we both belonged. He was also quick to call for organized opposition to the new organization set up by the Nazis, which all teachers were compelled to join. And it was Victor who knocked on my door one evening to present me with a statement he felt I ought to sign. It was my duty, he said. He placed a matchbox in my hand, and in this box I found a slip of paper. I bent my head over the paper and scanned it quickly.

> I hereby declare that I cannot take any part in
> the teaching of the young people of Norway
> according to the lines laid down by the German
> occupying force. . . . This would run counter to
> my own personal beliefs . . . forcing me to
> commit other acts that would conflict with my
> professional code of honor. . . . In all good
> conscience I must therefore state that I do not
> consider myself a member of the new teachers'
> union.

It was my duty, he said, running a hand through his thick fair hair—the very hand, it occurred to me, that my wife could not live without. And if I had an ounce of moral gumption, he went on, if I had ever wanted to show the world the kind of man—

I interrupted this tirade to point out that he was hardly in a position to be lecturing me on morality. To which he replied that I would have to set aside my personal—he hesitated for a moment—my personal failings; what was at issue here was something much bigger. I told him he hadn't changed a bit since the days when he was reciting bad poetry at the Trocadero. This was just more bad poetry. He nodded slowly.

"Am I to understand, Axel, that you won't sign it?"

"No, why on earth should I sign it?" I said. "One organization is as good as another. I'm a teacher, not a politician."

"And a magician," Victor added wryly, "with Quisling's blessing. You choose your friends with care."

"Yes, I am a magician. And, like I say, not a politician. I don't give a damn about any of this. I don't give a damn about anything you say, Victor, or anything you do."

I remember wondering where Gerd was. Sometimes she spent the night at his place. Was she there now? Was she waiting for him? Would they sit in his living room long into the night, laughing at me? I pulled myself together.

"It's time you were leaving," I said.

I led the way into the hall and opened the door. He followed but stopped in the doorway. He laid a hand on my arm. I pulled away.

"Do you want to talk about it?" he said.

"*Ha!*" I retorted.

"Is it that you're afraid?" he asked.

"Afraid? Afraid of what?"

"Afraid to sign the statement, afraid of what might happen if you did sign, afraid for yourself, for Gerd, and not least for little Alice?"

"Get out, Victor!"

"Because if that's so, if you are in fact afraid of signing, I'm here to tell you that you should be far more afraid of *not* doing so—"

"I've never felt less afraid," I snapped, cutting him off. "Goodbye!"

I pushed him out the door. He was heavier than I had expected, and a lot bigger. It took all my strength, but I eventually managed it. And then, with the door finally shut behind me, I dissolved, quite unexpectedly, into floods of tears.

When peace broke out, I knew it was only a matter of time before Gerd would want to leave me. Even so, when the word came I was quite unprepared. *Now listen to me, Axel, because this is going to hurt.* I was panic-stricken.

"*Axel Grutt, panic-stricken?*"

"*Yes, panic-stricken.*"

I did not want her to leave. I wanted her to stay with me. That was the only time I have ever really fought for something. And it turned me rotten inside. That fight left me rotten to the core. I heard myself threatening Gerd, saying I would take Alice away from her. I would have the law on my side, I reminded her. After all, hadn't she been neglecting house and home even before Alice was born, running off to Victor the way she did?

She was ready with her defense. "They won't take Alice away from me because of Victor," she said. "He's a war hero, Axel. And what are you?" She all but spat on the floor.

"I'll have the law on my side, Gerd. They'll take Alice away from you," I repeated. "They won't hesitate."

She came right up close to me, pressed her face against mine. "You don't even know for sure that she's yours," she hissed.

I stared at her, stunned. I raised my hand to hit her. "She's mine!" I roared. "Alice is my child. Don't do this, Gerd! Not this!"

And I sank down onto the sofa and howled. Gerd walked through to the bedroom and lay down on the bed. After a while I went in and lay down beside her. I stroked her face, her throat.

"Forgive me," I whispered. "Forgive me."

Stella Descending

She wept, hugged me, pressed herself close against me. I went on stroking her face. She grew soft in my arms. Her hands were all over me. *"Not so fast, Gerd, not so fast."* But she wasn't listening.

She was full of kisses.

I WAS PLANNING to watch the evening news at seven o'clock, but by the time I switch on the television the news is long since over. Everything has gone wrong today. It has all been too much. I take off my suit, unbutton my shirt, and hang everything in the closet. I set my shoes out in the hall, both my dress shoes and my sneakers. I take out a clean pair of pajamas, the ones with the blue stripes, and put them on. It is almost eleven o'clock. I shall sleep soon.

Often, before I go to bed, I listen to some of Schubert's piano music, but this evening I am more in the mood for song. I put on *Die Winterreise*. Luckily my half-deaf neighbor, the so-called music lover, is not at home. I haven't heard a sound from his apartment for days, maybe even weeks. It has been as quiet as can be in there. Maybe he's dead. Sometimes people just don't wake up from a good long night's sleep. I mean, where would he go? He had no friends. He never had any visitors, never went out. Well, I never! Maybe he really *is* dead. Bless him.

It is Fischer-Dieskau who is singing. I glance around the dark rooms. When I moved in here after Gerd's death, I brought nothing with me from the house we owned except the gilt mirror that hangs in the hall. I have never felt at home here. I've said it before and I'll say it again: I detest my surroundings, and my surroundings detest me. That is just how it is.

I sit down on the sofa. But then it is as if I got up again, crossed the room, and stood by the window.

So I stand there, looking at myself on the sofa, a little man sitting there all hunched up, so terribly alone. A bit of a poor soul, that one, I say to myself, and turn to look out the window. Suddenly it is snowing. Time has passed. It has been snowing for some days now. I lay my hand against the cold windowpane. A tram rolls past, almost empty, in the wintry gloom. Not the greatest of weather, if you ask me. I turn back to the poor soul on the sofa. Shall we have a cup of coffee, you and I?

I have lighted three candles: one for Gerd, one for Stella, and one for Amanda. I don't think Amanda will come here anymore. But if she should surprise me and ring the doorbell—I mean, if she should come over anyway, tomorrow, for example, or the next day—I could show her my barrel organ. She has never seen it. Fancy that. All the times she has visited me, and yet it has never occurred to me to show her the barrel organ. Granted, it's down in the cellar, so it would be quite a strain to lug it upstairs. But I could always ask someone to give me a hand. In my experience, people can be most obliging if you ask them for help. Take the young couple who've moved in next door, for instance. He's a conceited ass, anyone can see that, but she is graceful and charming, not unlike my daughter Alice when she was young. Alice, who could positively take my breath away simply by running down the street to meet me, with her arms outstretched. I am quite sure that if I were to ask that young couple to help Amanda and me carry the barrel organ up the stairs from the cellar, they would. I would offer them a cup of coffee afterward, naturally, and maybe some layer cake from the patisserie on the corner—as a way of saying thank-you for their trouble. It would be a nice gesture on my part. And after they'd gone,

Amanda and I would settle ourselves on the sofa and I would play for her.

"Funny old man," she'll say then, and I will see that she has her mother's eyes. "Can't I stay here with you a while?"

Amanda

The night is not far off. I've put Bee to bed and tucked her in. I got undressed, too, but I didn't get into bed. It's hot and I've pushed the window open as far as it can go. Before Bee fell asleep I said something I heard Mamma say to her once. I said, "It helps to cry."

But Bee shook her head.

So I said, "Well, it would help me if you cried."

She shook her head again.

You stupid kid! Our mother's dead and you just lie there. I felt like scratching her eyes out. Instead I patted her.

I said, "Have it your way, Bee, but there's always a chance that you'll wake up in the middle of the night and find me crying."

She nodded.

"Or maybe you'll wake up in the middle of the night and find I've gone for a walk. In which case, you just lie down and go back to sleep."

Several times, Martin opens the bedroom door and stands in the doorway looking at us, Bee under the covers and me still up.

"Put on your nightgown, Amanda," he whispers, "and shut that window. It's blowing a gale."

"Go away," I say.

The next time he looks in, he says exactly the same thing. "Put on your nightgown, Amanda, and shut that window. It's blowing a gale."

There are lots of things I don't tell Bee. For example: I might run away tonight. He might be waiting for me in town. We might climb some scaffolding, or a bell tower, or up onto a roof, just like Mamma and Martin, and we'll see the whole town spread out at our feet, and then we'll say *Snip, snap, snout* and he'll take me from behind, and at that moment I might actually catch fire.

But before that, before any of this, I'll sing five songs to Bee. I'll sing one for the old, one for the young, one for the living, and one for the dead. And then I'll sing one song just for you. D'you hear that, Bee? One song just for you. I want to be absolutely sure that you're asleep before I go.

The last time Martin looked in, he said, "Do you want to talk?"

I looked at him. "We're not friends, you and me. And don't you forget it!"

"Yeah, right," he said. "But put on your nightgown."

Corinne

It is a freezing winter's night, flurries of snow chased by rain in the deserted pitch-dark streets. The tram is almost empty. I am sitting right at the very back. A few seats in front of me sits a man, a stranger. There is something familiar about this stranger, my fellow passenger: his back maybe, or his hair, Bible-black. The tram stops and the man stands up to get off. I take the chance and call out to him. "Martin Vold, is that you?" The man turns, shakes his head, and smiles. It is not him. It is not Martin. This man has beady green eyes and a scar on his chin. I apologize for my mistake and we wish each other good night.

I have thought about Martin a lot lately. He dropped out of sight after Stella's funeral. I had completed my investigation, and he was not suspected of anything—or at least not anything that could be proved. He was free to do as he pleased, and he chose to disappear. My fellow officers and I were finished with him. Although it turns out that I was not, in fact, finished with him after all. I roam the city's streets like a woman in love, imagining that I see him on every corner. Not that I've ever been in love myself, heaven forbid! But in the course of my work I have come across enough women in love to know that this is pretty much how it affects them: Wherever they go they seem to see the face of their beloved—they see him getting into a car, leaning against a wall, at a café window, on the other side of the street.

Every now and then a face would present itself on the black shawl covering the window in Stella and Martin's bedroom. Martin said it was a woman's face. Stella said it was a man's. But they agreed that it was a face, and that the face spoke to them. They gave the face a name: Herr Poppel.

"Even though I was positive it was a woman's face, I went along with calling it Herr Poppel," Martin told me.

The date was September 2, 2000. Stella's funeral was only hours away. Martin and I were seated on either side of the big dining table. It would soon be morning.

"And what was Herr Poppel?" I asked. "What was his or her purpose?"

"She opened her big mouth and sang," said Martin.

"Sang?"

"Yes, sang," Martin repeated. "About us, Stella and me."

"And what did she sing on the last day of Stella's life?"

"Herr Poppel seldom sang during the day."

"I see. Okay, so what did Herr Poppel sing on the last night of Stella's life?"

"She sang a lullaby," said Martin. "The same lullaby that Stella used to sing to Bee when she was a baby. It was Stella who did the singing that night, too, in her deep Herr Poppel voice. She would lie beside me in bed, singing, until it got to the point where I had to ask her to shut up. I'd ask her to shut up, and she'd tell me it didn't pay to talk to Herr Poppel like that. I had to ask nicely, she'd say. So I'd ask nicely. 'Please, Herr Poppel, don't sing anymore tonight. And certainly not the song you're singing now, because it reminds me of weird little babies who never cry but keep us up all night just the same.' Stella would turn her back on me. 'Fuck you,' she would say. 'Fuck you, Martin.' Then we'd sleep back to back for a couple of hours."

"What time would you say you fell asleep the night before she died?"

"Past five, I guess," Martin said. "It took us all night to make the video for—"

"Ah, yes, the video," I said, interrupting him. "There was something I wanted to ask you. Several times on the video Stella says that there's something she wants to tell you."

"Does she? I don't remember."

"Did she tell you something that night?"

"I don't know."

"You don't know whether she told you anything?"

"No, I don't know. I can't think of anything in particular, if that's what you mean. But, no, I don't think so. Stella always had a hundred and one things buzzing around in her head, all of which she wanted to tell you. But there was nothing in particular. I would remember if there was."

"Might it have been that she was pregnant?"

"No."

"No, she didn't tell you she was pregnant, or no, she didn't tell you anything at all, or no, she wasn't pregnant?"

"No, no, no!"

I look at Martin. I say, "A yellowish mass, a bulge in the mucous membrane, a spongy little blob, an embryo less than a centimeter long."

This brings us to the last day.

Martin and Stella sleep back to back, and when they wake up a few hours later, the last day has already begun. Martin has given an account of this day many times already. He has spoken to my fellow officers, and he has spoken to me. So what do we have?

We have a man and a woman on the roof of an apartment building in Frogner, walking back and forth along the edge, like tightrope walkers, circus artistes, equilibrists. We have an embrace and a fall. The woman pulls herself out of the man's arms and falls. Or he pushes her and she falls. They are both tired, dead tired.

"An accident," the guys on the squad say. "It was their own fault, sure. They were irresponsible, sure. But it wasn't a crime. People who know them, and there aren't many, say their marriage wasn't that bad. Not that bad!"

"Any marriage that's not that bad is better than most marriages," say my fellow detectives. And I would have said the same, if I had not been bothered by this twinge in my stomach every time I sat face-to-face—

I broke my own train of thought. I said, "Let's go over it one more time, Martin."

Martin lit a cigarette, considered me. "Is that really necessary?"

"Is what necessary?"

"To go over it again? I liked it better when we were swapping stories."

"Let me remind you that I am here as a representative of the law and it ain't over till the fat lady sings."

"What do you want to know?"

"Everything. . . . Once upon a time, six days ago, Stella was still alive. The date is August 27, 2000."

"We woke up around eight," Martin said. "We were woken by the barking of the dog that never barks."

"Hoffa. Isn't that right?"

"Yes."

"Odd name for a dog."

"It was named after Jimmy Hoffa."

Martin looked around, as if expecting the dog to come bounding into the room.

"It's not here right now," he said. "I've packed it off somewhere."

I checked my notes. "So. The dog barked and you two woke up after sleeping for how long? Three hours?"

"Right, but there was nothing unusual about that. Many's

the time we didn't get any more sleep than that. I still dread sleep more than I dread sleeplessness."

Martin paused and lit a cigarette.

"Stella and I woke with a start and ran down the hall. Hoffa had shit all over the floor. He's a pathetic excuse for a dog. Have I mentioned that? The kind of dog you feel like hitting every time it lifts its head and looks at you. It's got those eyes. That sort of look in them. It expects to be beaten, and it would never occur to it to bite back. And on this particular morning it had done its business in the hall, and there it was, standing at the door, barking. We woke up and everything was . . . turned upside down. Nothing was as it should be. We were both staggering around like sleepwalkers. I tried unsuccessfully to rub the sleep from my eyes. Stella was feeling nauseated and had to make a sudden dash for the bathroom to throw up. It was sultry, hot, sunny, and stifling. The dog that never barked was barking. There was shit all over the floor. The church bells were ringing. It was Sunday and the church bells were ringing. Amanda came running down the stairs, her hair all mussed up and her cheeks blotchy. She had pulled on a crumpled white T-shirt. Her legs were long and brown, her breasts were full. 'What's going on?' she whispered to Stella. 'What's going on?' 'I'm feeling nauseous,' Stella said. We all stood there in the hall, surrounded by piles of dog shit, Amanda, Stella, and me—and the dog. Bee was missing. That's why the dog was barking. Bee had gone out without the dog. She always walked the dog in the morning. It was her dog. Her responsibility. But now she was missing.

"It didn't take us long to find her. She was standing outside our next-door neighbors' house in her blue nightgown, gazing into their garden. She's all eyes, that child! On the other side of the fence, two girls were jumping on a trampoline. Up and down, up and down, up and down. They're Bee's classmates, these two. Although *mates* is hardly the right word. A few months back these same girls had kicked Hoffa in the belly. The dog hadn't quite been itself since. The girls' kicking left its mark on Bee, too. Now and then she would just disappear, and when she did we usually found her exactly the way we found her this time, standing outside our neighbors' garden gate, staring, Bee on one side of the fence and the girls on the other. Up and down, up and down, up and down on the trampoline. It's a strange summertime sight, this: children bouncing up and down on a trampoline. None of us, not Stella, not Amanda, not I, could tear ourselves away from the sight of these two girls bouncing up and down."

Martin lit a cigarette.

"We were quite a sight ourselves," he says. "A family of four with a pathetic dog in tow, standing outside the neighbors' garden gate. All of us in our night things, all four with messed-up hair, and all four"—Martin thought for a moment—"all four of us down for the count. That's the only way I can put it. We were knocked out, licked. We'd lost the war. We were refugees in a strange land. When the mother of one of the girls on the trampoline caught sight of us through an open French window and came toward us with a steaming cup of tea in her hand, we didn't stir. We stood outside her garden gate, huddled together like a bunch of ragamuffins. She came closer, her head tilted to the side. 'What are you doing there? What do you want? Why aren't you at home? What are doing out here in your night things?'

"Suddenly Stella seemed to come to life. She cleared her throat. She pointed at the two girls on the trampoline.

"'Those two girls kicked my daughter's dog,' she said quietly, 'and I think they ought to apologize.'

"The trampoline girl's mother looked flabbergasted.

"'But Stella,' she said, lingering over the name, 'we sorted all that out months ago. The dog was loose, the girls were afraid . . . none of us can say exactly what happened, can we?'

"The trampoline girl's mother cast a perplexed glance at Bee, as if to say, And we can't believe anything she says, that's for sure.

"'I know exactly what happened,' Stella said drowsily. She had almost fallen asleep again, asleep on her feet there, outside the neighbors' garden gate, giving up with a sigh. She had been like this ever since that time she was sick: a fleeting spark, soon snuffed.

"'Oh, who cares,' she muttered.

"She turned her back on the woman.

"'Come on,' she said to us. She took Bee by the hand and started to walk away.

"Amanda, the dog, and I turned away, too, and followed her home.

"The rest of that day passed in a dreamlike haze," Martin told me. "Stella and I slept a lot, couldn't seem to wake up properly. The black shawl fluttered gently over the bedroom window. Before, Stella always used to insist on taking the shawl down during the day, to let the light in. But we never took it down now. It hung over the window, pinned there by four thumbtacks, one blue, two red, and one yellow. We could hear the Nintendo in Amanda's room. Bee had curled up in the basket with the dog. They often lay like that, those two, the dog with his leg over Bee or Bee with her arm around the dog. All was quiet, not a sound except for the relentless *piip-piip-tjoom-piip-piip-tjoom* from Amanda's room. Stella and I lay hand in hand on the bed, on top of the eiderdown, staring at the ceiling.

"'Listen to how quiet it is,' she said.

"'Hmmm.' I grunted and drowsed on.

"'You'd never believe there was a family living in this house,' she said. 'With children and all.'

"I yawned.

"'It's not natural.'

"A gentle breeze was blowing outside. The black shawl over the window rose and fell.

"'Look, there's Herr Poppel,' Stella said, propping herself up on her elbows.

"'Yep,' I said, 'there she is.'

"Then the rain started.

"We fell asleep eventually," Martin said. "We fell asleep when the rain came. It's so nice to be lulled to sleep by the sound of rain. The kids were used to our sleeping during the day when we weren't at work, so they didn't disturb us. After a while, though, Bee did wander through to our room.

"'Mamma,' she said.

"'Let me sleep,' Stella murmured.

"'But I've got something to tell you,' Bee said.

"'Later, honey,' said Stella.

"Then Stella reached out her arms and pulled Bee onto the bed.

"'Why don't you snuggle up here with me for a little while,' she whispered. 'And we'll have a nice nap here, all three of us.'

"When we woke up again, maybe a half hour later, it was still raining. Bee had gone in to Amanda. We were alone in the room. We chatted about this and that. Stella reminded me of the time I delivered the sofa and almost jumped out her ninth-floor window. Then she started to cry.

"'I wish we could start all over again,' she sobbed. 'I wish you were standing outside my window again. I wish we could celebrate your grandmother's seventy-fifth birthday again. I wish we could have Bee again. More than anything else, I wish that we could have . . . I don't like all this silence.'

"I stroked her hair. I wasn't exactly sure what she wanted from me, so I said, 'Would you like me to sing to you?'

"So I sang to Stella," Martin said. "Songs she liked. Songs I had sung to her when she was sick. Songs that made her happy."

"I didn't know you could sing," I said.

"When I was a little boy my grandmother Harriet used to sing to me. Stella didn't like Harriet. But she softened slightly toward her when I told the story of how my grandfather ran off and left her in the lurch when she was a young girl with a baby on the way. She had heard that story a thousand times before, but all at once she seemed to be listening to it in a different way. My grandfather fell in love with an actress, I told her. Loved her from afar, that is. Fell in love, not just with her but with his own dreams of stardom. Farming wasn't for him, and he couldn't have cared less about Grandma or the child she was carrying.

"Suddenly Stella sat up in bed and said, 'Hey, the sun's come out. Let's go get everyone something nice to eat.'

"That was fine by me, so we jumped out of bed. We told the kids we were going out to pick up something for dinner and wouldn't be gone long. We drove past the apartment block on Frognerplass where we had lived in the early days, and I said, 'Wasn't it you who said you'd like to start all over again?'

"'Uh-huh,' Stella said hesitantly.

"'Well, that's easily arranged,' I said.

"'No games now, Martin,' Stella pleaded. 'I'm hungry. The kids are waiting for us.'

"But I wasn't listening to her. I parked the car. Dragged her out of the passenger seat and up to the front door. I asked her if she remembered the view from the roof. She nodded. We used to go out on the roof in the old days; there was a skylight we could climb through.

"'Know what?' I said. 'We're going back up on that roof.'

"She nodded again.

"We didn't have to wait too long before someone let himself out of the building and we seized the chance to slip through the door. We took the stairs, not the elevator."

All this time, Martin had been running something through his fingers. It was a little silver locket.

"I can't explain it any other way," Martin said, "except to say that something happened to us up there on the roof. We woke up. We became our old selves again. Maybe it was the view, maybe it was that giddy feeling, maybe it was the thought that we could actually start over. We teetered back and forth, back and forth, along the edge of the roof. Daring each other, just like we had done that time in the store when Stella's water broke and Bee was on the way and everything changed. It was a game. It wasn't in earnest. It was a game. Then we turned to face each other. I opened my arms and she wavered toward me, taking little bitty steps like a tightrope walker. I once saw a tightrope walker dancing along her rope on tiptoe, a pink parasol in one hand and the hem of her dress in the other. That's how Stella looked, like a doll, sort of like a doll, and we stood there, wrapped in each other's arms, and Stella whispered to me that from now on everything was going to be fine.

"'I'm not a tree,' she said, 'and it really is possible; it really is possible to start all over again.' We both gazed up at the sky, and it was exactly like lying on the grass on a summer's evening, staring at the drifting clouds, and Stella laughed, let go of me, and pointed to a blue cloud shaped like a face, with a nose, forehead, two or three eyes, and a big mouth, and she said, 'Look, Martin, there's Herr Poppel.'"

Stella Descending

Video Recording: Stella & Martin
The House by the Lady Falls
8/27/00, 5:55 A.M.

MARTIN: I can hear someone tramping on the stairs. Who's that tramping on my stairs? Could it be Amanda? No, Amanda is asleep. Could it be Bee? No, Bee is asleep. Could it be the plumber? No, the plumber is asleep. Could it be Stella?

STELLA: Martin, put that camera down.

MARTIN: This is Stella. My wife. More beautiful than beautiful. She got mad at me a little while ago and stormed upstairs. Now she's back. Nice to see you, Stella. Greetings from Mr. Insurance Agent Gunnar R. Owesen and myself.

STELLA: Martin! Put that camera down!

MARTIN: But we're not finished.

STELLA: We're not?

MARTIN: No, Stella, we're not.

STELLA: Put that camera down and come to bed. It's almost morning.

MARTIN: Take the camera for a moment.

STELLA: Okay. Now what?

MARTIN: What do you see, Stella?

STELLA: I see your face.

MARTIN: And what do you say?

STELLA: I say, This is Martin. My husband. He has blue eyes, although sometimes when he thinks no one is watching him, his eyes are almost green. On his chin he has a little sore spot that never heals. Right now he is sitting on the avocado-green sofa, staring at the ceiling. I wonder what he's thinking. Maybe he's not thinking about anything. Maybe he's thinking about me. Maybe he's thinking that everything has turned to ashes. That we all went up in flames anyway.

MARTIN: Stella, put the camera down and let's go to bed.

STELLA: Say good night to Mr. Insurance Agent Gunnar R. Owesen!

MARTIN: Good night, Gunnar R. Owesen.

STELLA: Good night, Gunnar R. Owesen.

MARTIN: Sleep tight. And sweet dreams.

(V)

FALL

When I lost my footing and fell toward the ground, I flung my long arms around my tummy and said, Now we're flying, you and I. You're no bigger than a fingernail. You're a bulge in the mucous membrane, a spongy little blob, an excrescence. You have unlimited depths. You could be anyone you wanted to be. Even a tree, if you set your mind to it. Although I wouldn't recommend it. I've known a few trees in my time, and they don't have much to say for themselves. Me, I get nervous around trees. My body rumbles and roars and leaves its mark wherever it goes. It's embarrassing. There were times when I too wished I were a tree, a body that left no trace of itself behind. But things didn't work out that way. I bled. I laughed. When I was expecting Amanda I used to wonder what sort of face she would have. That, to me, was the greatest mystery of all. Not only was I going to have a baby, but that baby would have a face. And when I was expecting Bee, I wondered what sort of face she would have. And now it's your turn.

Now it's your turn.

You are the mystery.

And someday, very soon, I will give you a name.

A NOTE ABOUT THE AUTHOR

Born in 1966, Linn Ullmann is a graduate of New York University, where she studied English literature and began work on a Ph.D. She returned to Oslo in 1990 to pursue a career in journalism. She had established herself as a prominent literary critic when her first novel, *Before You Sleep*, was published in 1998 and became a critically acclaimed best-seller throughout Europe. She writes a column for Norway's leading morning newspaper and lives in Oslo with her husband, son, two stepchildren, and a dog.

A NOTE ON THE TYPE

The text of this book was set in a typeface called Bell. The original punches for this face were cut in 1788 by the engraver Richard Austin for the type-foundry of John Bell (1745–1831), the most outstanding typographer of his day. They are the earliest English "modern" type design, and show the influence of French copperplate engraving and the work of the Fournier and Didot families. However, the Bell face has a distinct identity of its own, and might also be classified as a delicate and refined rendering of Scotch Roman.

Composed by
Stratford Publishing Services,
Brattleboro, Vermont

Printed and bound by
R. R. Donnelley & Sons,
Harrisonburg, Virginia

Designed by
Soonyoung Kwon

		DATE DUE	

9/03

FICTION